ELLA AND HER SHIFTERS

ARIA WINTER

JADE WALTZ

Purple Fall
Publishing

Published in the United States by Purple Fall Publishing. Purple Fall Publishing and the Purple Fall Publishing Logos are trademarks and/or registered trademarks of Purple Fall Publishing LLC.-purplefallpublishing.com

Publisher's Cataloging-in-Publication data

Names: Winter, Aria, author. | Waltz, Jade, author.

Title: Ella And Her Shifters : A Reverse Harem Shifter Romance / Aria Winter & Jade Waltz.

Series: Once Upon a Shifter

Description: Purple Fall Publishing, 2021.

Identifiers: ISBN:

978-1-64253-004-9 (pbk.)

978-1-64253-512-9 (ebook)

978-1-64253-009-4 (audiobook)

Subjects: LCSH Shapeshifting--Fiction. | Magic--Fiction. | Man-woman relationships--Fiction. | Love stories. | Paranormal fiction. | Paranormal romance stories. | Science fiction. | BISAC FICTION / Romance / Paranormal | FICTION / Romance / Science Fiction

Classification: PS3623 .I6675 E45 2021 | DDC 813.6--dc23

Cover Design by Samantha Rose at Rose Cover Designs

https://www.facebook.com/rosecoverdesigns/

PRINTED IN THE UNITED STATES OF AMERICA

Cover Design by Samantha Rose at Rose Cover Designs

https://www.facebook.com/rosecoverdesigns/

PRINTED IN THE UNITED STATES OF AMERICA

Dedication

To my husband: Thank you for all your love and support. You are not just my husband, you are my best friend and my rock. I love you more than anything.

-Aria Winter

To My Husband,
Thank you for being my support and rock during this writing journey. I love you!

-Jade Waltz

CHAPTER 1

ELLA

Shifters are myths—the villains of every cautionary tale told to children. But not according to my father. He used to claim he knew them, and they were real. He convinced me he could speak to them in their animal forms.

We used to picnic in the forest, and he would pretend to talk to birds, squirrels, chipmunks, and rabbits. I was completely captivated by the tales he'd weave as he supposedly communed with them. I suppose that's why the forest sitting on the estate has always been a place of wonder and magic for me—a forbidden sanctuary I was no longer allowed to wander.

Once, I even imagined I saw a fox shift into a human, but in a blink of an eye, they were gone.

Now that I am older, I realize that was simply the product of an overactive imagination because I believed in my father's wild stories of mythical creatures and the humans that had befriended them.

He told me that on my eighteenth birthday, I'd inherit the gift that's passed down through our bloodline and that I'd be able to speak with them too. It's been several years since my father passed, leaving me with my stepmother and her two daughters: Mary and Beth. They would think me foolish for coming here today, but they don't understand the pain of loss like I do.

I suppose I should thank them, however. With all the hard labor they've forced me to do over the years, I've had very little time to lose myself to my grief. It's only on days like today where it is especially painful and reminds me that I was born into this world to people who loved me. The only ones who cared, but are now gone.

As I make my way down the overgrown path, following it to the clearing where we used to have our picnics, I do not expect to be able to magically communicate with animals just because today is my eighteenth birthday. No. I come here today simply to honor and remember my father, knowing that if he were alive now, he would probably insist upon us coming here too.

I wore my finest dress. The one made of pale blue fabric that matches my eyes and a golden sash to compliment my light blond hair.

As I pass beneath the great trees of the forest, I speculate that they have been here hundreds of years from their sheer size. Branches thick with leaves weave together overhead, creating a dense canopy that blocks most of the light from the sun.

Some would think it is romantic, being able to hide from the world with their significant other. Perhaps even taking the time to carve their initials in one of the nearby tree trunks. I often wonder how it feels to be in such a relationship like I've read in books, to have someone love you so much that they are willing to do anything to make you happy.

But that isn't my life, nor do I have time to daydream of such things, not when my time is filled doing chores.

Despite the canopy's near darkness, I am not scared, unlike my stepsisters who fear going even near the forest line. In a way, I feel safe, knowing that they won't follow me here.

Smiling brightly, I watch the wildlife as they continue with their daily routine as I press on, knowing the clearing is just up ahead.

Although it has been several years, it is precisely as I remember. The wild grass that blankets the ground is spongy beneath my feet from the almost constant rains we've had over the past several days. Small, purple flowers dot the landscape. Their sweet fragrance drifting on the cool breeze as I lay out my blanket.

The tattered and worn cloth has seen better days, but it's the only thing I could find that my stepmother wouldn't miss. Technically, I'm supposed to be repolishing the floors in the guest wing right now, but I doubt she'll notice I'm not there. After my father died, she has spent most of her time away from the estate, fraternizing with influential lords, ladies, and all manner of wealthy merchants as she tries to climb the social ladder. I often wonder if my father was just a step or if she had actually loved him.

I want to believe that they were in love.

I'll have plenty of time to finish my chores once I return, especially since I did some extra ones for a week prior to today, knowing that I would be taking the whole morning off once she left. I usually don't get a chance to venture out into the forest, so I'm going to make the best of it while I'm here.

It's my birthday; I deserve to have a small break.

Besides, who's going to discover me out here?

ARIA WINTER & JADE WALTZ

With a wistful sigh, I pull a wrapped parcel from my dress pocket and carefully unfold the small napkin. A thick slice of bread with honey smeared across the face is the best I could do on short notice for a birthday cake for myself.

I lift it to the sky, wondering if my mother and father are watching over me even now. "Happy birthday to me," I mutter to no one as I imagine my parents looking down and smiling upon me.

I open my mouth to take a small bite but stop when I notice two chipmunks making their way toward me. Their striped-copper fur bodies fail to hide them against the summer brush, and I'm surprised that they appear so unafraid.

"Why, hello!" I smile brightly at them, pretending as my father once did that I could speak to animals. "I'm so glad you're here."

They sit on their back legs and stare up at me with bright green eyes that seem to study me curiously.

"Would you like some bread?"

I break off two small pieces, set them before the chipmunks, and watch as they eagerly begin to eat.

Did the sweet honey scent of my treat attract them? Or was it their curiosity that brought them over?

I don't ponder it now; I'm just glad that they're here. My days, typically filled with loneliness, makes me appreciate their company. I lie back on the blanket and pull the small book from my pocket that I've been reading of late. It's nothing new. I have read it several times before, but I always enjoy the story nonetheless. It's about a girl with an evil stepmother who is a witch. She ends up being saved by a prince in the end, and they get married.

Perhaps that's why I love this one so much. It's what I often wish could happen to me. I sigh as I stare up at the puffy white

4

clouds overhead. "Wouldn't it be wonderful if I could fall in love with the prince, and he'd take me away from my evil step-mother and cherish and protect me for the rest of my life?"

The chipmunks lie on the blanket beside me while I read, chattering to each other. I frown in disappointment that I cannot understand what they're saying. Part of me had hoped my father wasn't lying because it would be positively magical if I could communicate with animals.

It's strange that they trust me so readily, but maybe it's because I gave them food. I do my best not to disturb them as they curl up next to me. I smile down at them and speak softly. "I'm glad you're here. I don't want you to leave. It's not often that I have company."

They lift their heads to look up at me, and a man's voice speaks in my mind. *"Then, we will stay."*

Stunned, I blink down at them. Am I going crazy? "Did you... did you just—"

I don't get to finish my question because a nearby low growl startles me.

I jerk my head up to see a pair of amber eyes blinking at me from the darkness of the forest. Goosebumps prickle my flesh. I cannot make out what kind of creature it is, but it stares at me with a predatory gaze. My heart stops and then begins hammering as the large shadow stalks closer.

Cautiously, I get to my feet. I'm not sure if I should run or stay still. My every nerve ending hums in acute awareness and anticipation, my body primed to fight or to run.

As I struggle with my indecision, ice fills my veins as the predator steps into the clearing. With a thick coat of dark gray fur and a long black tail, it bares two rows of sharp fangs, dripping with saliva. The wolf's gaze holds mine, its lips pulled back in a feral snarl as a low growl rumbles in its chest.

"You are Ella." A man's voice speaks low and menacingly in my head. *"You are the one we seek."*

My mouth drifts open. "Are you talking to me?"

"Yes."

"I—I don't understand. How are you able to speak in my mind?"

The wolf's eyes bore into mine as it steps closer.

The chipmunks move in front of me. I watch in shock as they transform into two humans in the blink of an eye.

Instantly, their fur and tails disappear, revealing two handsome men with golden skin and light brown hair. Layers of thick, corded muscle line their arms and legs. They are bare-chested and wearing some sort of loincloth tied loose around their waist. They are taller than any men I've seen before, and their shoulders are broad. As my gaze travels over their bodies, I realize that they're twins. With square jaws, heavy-set brows, and aristocratic features, the only resemblance to their animal form is their green eyes.

Without warning, the wolf lunges toward them.

A scream rips from my throat as their bodies collide with the predator, the crashing sound like an axe splitting wood.

I observe in stunned silence as they fight the wolf. It clamps its jaws around the first one's arm. He releases an inhuman roar as he punches at its snout to break free. The second man wraps his arms around its chest trying to pull it away from his brother.

The wolf cries out in pain, releasing his hold. I watch in shock as the man wraps his hands on either side of its face and twists.

A horrible crack slices through the air and the wolf goes still, collapsing to the ground in a crumpled heap. I stare in disbelief as its dead body shifts into that of a naked man with dark hair.

I turn my gaze to the two men. Panic fills me as my eyes rake over the many deep cuts and claw marks across their arms and bare chests. Each of them heavily wounded and bleeding. We're far from the estate and any help. I'm surprised they are still able to stand. Panting heavily, they stare down at their kill in disgust.

"What just—" The rest of my question dies in my throat as one of the men collapses.

Despite my shock, I rush toward him and drop to my knees. I cup his cheek, turning his face to me. "Are you all right?"

His brother kneels beside us, concern evident in his green eyes. "Finn, how badly are you hurt?"

Finn winces as he looks up at his brother. "I... I should be better soon." He barely manages. "Cash, you need to protect her in case there are more." He places his hand over mine and closes his eyes as his head falls back.

Panic tightens my chest. I whip my head toward his brother. "We need to find help!"

Cash looks to me, his face lacking the concern that I feel. "He'll be fine. We just need to find a safe and quiet place for him to recover."

I blink at him in shock. My gaze darts to the deep cuts that mar Finn's forearms and chest. Compared to Cash, it's easy to see that he took most of the blows during the fighting. "He's heavily injured. We need to get him to a healer. Now."

Cash meets my eyes evenly. "Trust me. He will heal on his own. He just needs time. Do you have somewhere we can take him? Somewhere safe?"

The way his eyes scan the forest as if looking for any signs of danger sends a chill down my spine. Before he passed out, Finn warned there could be more wolves. I certainly don't want to stay here to find out if he was right.

Swallowing thickly, I push down my fear and force myself to focus. "Yes. We should go back to the estate."

"Lead the way." Cash carries Finn's unconscious form as he follows behind me. I'm surprised by his strength and how easily he keeps pace with me despite his heavy burden.

I call out over my shoulder, "When we get there, I'll send for the town's healer."

Cash shakes his head. "That won't be necessary. He will heal. We just need somewhere safe for him to do it."

I give him a wary look as we make our way out of the forest and back up the path to the estate. "I can't help but notice you keep saying we need to get somewhere 'safe.' What do you mean? Are you worried there are more—" I pause, struggling to find the right word to describe what I saw, finally I settle upon "creatures like that wolfman back in the woods."

"Yes," Cash replies, his face hardening. "That, or something much worse."

"There are worse things than that?" I ask incredulously.

"Unfortunately, there are. But you do not have to worry Ella. We will protect you."

"You will?" I hate the small squeak in my voice as I ask, but I'm still so shaken by what I just witnessed, I cannot help it.

"Yes," he replies solemnly. "With our lives."

A disturbing realization hits me. I meet his gaze evenly. "How do you know my name? And why aren't you more worried about your brother?"

A grin tilts his lips. "Trust me. He's been injured far worse than this and recovered just fine. And as for your name... we came here to find you."

I blink at him, astonished. "Why me?"

"It's... a lot to explain," he says, and I note the hesitation in his tone. "Once we're somewhere safe, I promise I will tell you everything."

"All right." Strange as it may seem, I trust him. After all, he and his brother saved my life. If they hadn't intervened, I'd probably be dead right now. And if they had meant me any harm, they could have done whatever they wanted to me in the forest. No one would have ever known.

I glance back over my shoulder again at Cash, carrying his brother. Myriad questions run through my mind but they'll have to wait for later. Right now, I just want to get as far away from the woods as possible and hope nothing follows us.

I lead him up the side path to the estate gardens. Quickly, we move past all the flower and vegetable beds, skirting around the large fountain in the center. As we move past the tomatoes, I recall how only yesterday I picked several ripe ones to use for a stew. Back before I realized that shifters actually existed.

I lead Cash toward the tower in the far corner. It's connected to the main house, but you wouldn't know it from the state of disrepair. The worn and heavy wooden door creaks on its hinges despite my attempt to open it quietly. My gaze travels up the spiraling staircase that leads to my room at the top.

I look over my shoulder to the brothers. "We can take him to my room, but it's at the top of the tower. Can you make it with him like that?"

"Of course." Cash says this as if carrying a full-grown man, almost his exact size is nothing. I'm surprised as he follows me up the winding staircase with ease, especially since I still trip every so often from the worn and uneven steps.

Wind howls throughout the structure from the many missing stones and broken windows as we ascend. I do my best to keep it all neat and tidy, but I lack the means to repair any of these things. Still, I suppose I should be grateful for its current state. If it were pristine like the rest of the main house, my stepmother would surely have relegated me to the stables instead of allowing me to keep my room here.

As soon as we reach my room, I note the stunned look on Cash's face as he takes it all in. "This... is your room?"

"Yes."

When his gaze meets mine, sadness and pity are easily read in his expression, but he says nothing further.

I motion for him to lay Finn down on my bed. It's little more than a straw pallet covered with fabric, but at least it's clean and somewhat softer than the hard wooden floor. Unfortunately, I don't have much in the way of furniture. Only a small table and chairs in one corner and a torn sofa that my stepmother was going to throw out, but I salvaged before she got rid of it.

I quickly move to the water basin and grab a clean towel from beside it, bringing it over to him. I kneel next to Finn, and my jaw drops. He's completely naked.

I blink up at Cash. "What happened to his clothes?"

He gives me an apologetic look. "It is hard to maintain the appearance of clothing when we are injured."

I frown in confusion. "The... what?"

He opens his mouth to reply, but Finn groans low in his throat, drawing my attention back to him. "Finn?" I speak his name, but he doesn't answer.

Blood seeps steadily from the five jagged marks across his torso from the wolf's claws. The cuts on his arms aren't nearly as deep, but they're still worrisome. I dip the clean cloth in the water and drag it over his skin to cleanse the wounds, trying but failing to keep my eyes from drifting lower. I've never seen a man naked before, and I'm shocked by how big he is. Not just his muscles and body, but his manhood.

I've heard women in the town refer to this part of a man as his "length," but they failed to mention the girth as well.

Averting my gaze, I lift the tattered blanket that I use as a comforter and drape it over his lower half to keep my eyes from wandering where they shouldn't. After all, it's not proper to view a man without clothing unless he is one's husband.

Cash kneels beside me, and I'm glad, at least, that *he* is still wearing pants.

I force myself to focus on cleaning Finn's wounds. My mouth drifts open as I notice the torn tissue beginning to knit back together before my eyes. "How is that possible?"

"We heal very quickly."

I scan Cash's body and notice that his wounds are now slowly healing as well. "What exactly... are you?"

His warm, green eyes meet mine as he takes my hand gently in his own. "I know this is a bit of a shock to you, Ella, but we are shifters."

"Shifters." I breathe the word out as my mind struggles to wrap around the concept I believed only this morning to be no more than a myth. "And the wolf in the woods?"

He dips his chin in a subtle nod. "The same, just a different animal."

My brow furrows. "Why chipmunks?" I ask, the thought suddenly striking me as odd.

"The smaller one is, the better one can observe the world and everyone around them unnoticed. Don't you agree?" Cash's lips curve up in a sly grin. "Besides, I was born into it. Our parents were the same. If our parents had been wolf shifters, Finn and I would be as well."

I nod because as impossible as this all sounds, that makes sense. "And there are... more of you?"

"Yes." He chuckles, amusement dancing behind his eyes. "We are many."

Finn makes another noise, and I reach down to gently stroke his cheek. "Are you awake? How do you feel?"

Finn gently places his hand over mine as his eyelids flutter open. His green eyes stare up at me, and he gives me a weak smile. "I am feeling much better. Thank you, Ella. You are very kind."

For all I've heard tales of shifters being dangerous, these two don't instill any sense of fear in me. I don't know why, but I feel that I can trust them.

I don't, however, know how others would receive them. I suspect it would be with much fear and suspicion. People tend to be afraid of things they don't understand, and this would certainly qualify as such.

I smile back at Finn. "Thank you for saving me." I look between the two of them. "Both of you. And don't worry, I will speak to no one of your... abilities."

Finn gives me a faint grin. "Thank you, Ella."

I run the cloth over his skin again, glad when I notice his wound is now completely closed over. Only slight pink marks remain where the deep cuts and gashes had been mere moments ago. A thought suddenly occurs to me. "I'll go find you some clothing."

He shakes his head. "There is no need."

I frown. "You cannot walk around naked."

Finn pulls back the tattered comforter and is now magically wearing pants. They don't do much to conceal what I saw earlier. In fact, if anything, the outline of his pants only makes his manhood more noticeable.

He sits up, his face mere inches from me. A warm flush creeps up my neck, to my cheeks. A grin tugs at his lips, curving into a devastatingly handsome smile as his intense green gaze holds mine. He's the most attractive man I've ever met before. Him and his brother.

They are masculine perfection made manifest before me, and I'm embarrassed by the sudden arousal blooming deep within.

I don't understand my reaction. It's not as if I haven't been around handsome men before. But something about these two fills me with a desire that is as surprising as it is overwhelming.

I force myself to avert my gaze. "Are you hungry?"

"Yes."

"Wait here." I press down on Finn's chest to push him onto his back. "You should lie down. You're still healing," I gently chastise. "I will be right back."

I rush down the stairs to the kitchen and nearly run into the delivery man. "Your supplies are here, Ella."

"Oh. Thank you."

He grins, revealing a mouth full of several missing teeth. Each time I see him, he seems to have fewer and fewer. Poor man. I force myself to look up at his eyes, not wanting to stare. "Have you heard the news, Ella? The palace just announced a royal ball."

"A ball?"

"Yes. And all eligible, unmarried women in the kingdom are required to attend."

That's... strange. "Why is that?"

He chuckles. "It seems the prince is in need of a wife."

Hope fills me. "All unmarried women?" I ask, just to be sure I've heard correctly.

"Yes."

My thoughts drift to my story about the prince who saved the girl from her evil stepmother. I can imagine how lovely such a thing would be: to be chosen by the prince and to live happily ever after, away from this life of indentured servitude that I've endured since my father died.

My stepmother took everything out from under me after his passing. Apparently, the authorities were quite happy to take her coin and look the other way as she cheated me out of my father's will. She claimed she was doing it because I was not yet of age to attend to such things. Now that I am older, I know the truth.

I thank the delivery man and pay him his coin.

As I head for the kitchen to retrieve something for Finn, I wonder when my stepfamily will return. They went into the town earlier, and I'm sure they must have already heard the royal announcement about the ball. I imagine once they hear of it, they'll probably spend a fortune on new dresses.

I have asked many times to have my rights to my father's fortune back, but Griselda always has an excuse for why she still needs to handle everything for me. Unfortunately, I'm reasonably certain that she's gone through most of the money my father left behind by now.

She says I should be grateful. That most orphans are tossed out onto the streets once their parents have died. I suppose I should be. At least, she cares enough not to have done that to me. Even if she and her daughters treat me like a servant, they still provide for me in a way. Without them, I'd have nowhere to go.

However, I can't stop thinking about the royal ball. I'm glad for the material I've saved over the years. Most of it is scrap left behind by dressmakers when they've come to fit my stepsisters, but it's enough to make something beautiful to wear to such an occasion, I'm sure.

As I search the kitchen for something for Finn and Cash, a familiar voice calls out. Dread trickles down my spine when I recognize the impatient tone of my stepmother.

CHAPTER 2

ELLA

My stepmother stares down at me with a thunderous expression. "Where were you?"

"I was repolishing the floors in the guest wing," I lie. She doesn't need to know what happened. I'm not even sure I entirely understand it myself. Besides, she couldn't have been home that long, or she would've been curious about who was at the door earlier when the delivery man came.

A sharp slap across my cheek knocks me back, and I hit the wall, banging my head sharply against it. I barely manage to stay on my feet as I grip the table beside me to steady myself. I place my hand to my face, as if that will somehow ease the sting, and lift my eyes to her in confusion.

"Do not lie to me!" she snaps. "I went to the guest wing to find you, and you weren't there." She gives me an icy glare. "Now. Tell me the truth."

I open my mouth, not sure how much to tell her. After a moment, I decide to tell her where I was and not what happened. Besides, I doubt she'd believe me anyway. "I went to the forest. It's my birthday," I offer, cautiously. "I went to the place where Father used to take me to picnic when I was a child. Do you remember? When you were first married, you went with us as well."

Her expression softens as she stares down at me. In my heart, I believe she did have love for my father, but he died so soon after their marriage there just wasn't enough time for her to have felt much for me. Sometimes I wonder if she was upset at me because I always had reminded my late father of my mother, his first love, and how he lost her.

Yet I never understood how my stepmother could be so jealous of my late mother. I remember how in love they seemed shortly after their marriage. She had definitely captured my father's heart.

"You know it's dangerous out there." She eyes my wrinkled dress. "Even for a girl such as yourself."

Normally, I would argue. But this time, she's right.

I could have been killed today. If it weren't for the shifter twins, I would have.

She shakes her head and gives me a pitying look. Reaching out, she cups my cheek tenderly. The same one she just slapped not even a minute ago. The echoes of remembered pain whisper across my still stinging flesh. "My dear, sweet girl. You know nothing of this world. That's why you must take great care and be cautious at all times. I wouldn't want anything terrible to happen to you."

She stares at me with something akin to concern in her eyes. It's moments like these that confuse me. Sometimes I think she hates me, but then she goes and says something like this. Something that almost sounds like what a mother would say to her child.

I lower my eyes, afraid she will strike me again believing I am trying to challenge her. "You're right, Stepmother. I will be more careful." Remembering what I'd heard from the delivery man, I lift my gaze to her again. "The delivery man had exciting news today."

She arches a brow, as if trying to suppress her interest in what I have to say, but she doesn't fool me. I know she loves news and gossip just as much as her daughters.

I continue. "The palace issued a decree. They are hosting a royal ball. All eligible maidens are required to attend."

"I heard that this morning as well." She rolls her eyes, unimpressed by my news. "Everyone has heard of this by now."

I do my best to ignore her comment and walk to the linen closet where I've stored all the fabric I've saved. I want to go to the ball, and I know she'll only agree if I already have the material I need to make a dress for myself. She certainly would not think of buying anything for me. "I... I saved this material and fabric." I hold it out to her. "And I have enough to make myself a dress, and to possibly make a sash or some kind of trim for Mary and Beth as well if they'd like."

Her eyes search mine a moment, narrowing. She reaches out and takes the fabric from me, rubbing it between her thumb and forefinger as she studies it closely. "No." She sniffs. "This will not do for Mary or Beth. But it should suit you just fine."

I'm not quite sure how to respond since it is the very same fabric they've had dresses made from over the years, so instead, I just nod.

"Ella?"

"Yes?"

She gives me a thin-lipped smile. "We're going out this evening. You needn't make any dinner."

A noise at the top of the stairs draws my attention. I look up to find Mary and Beth dressed in matching gowns with their hair braided exactly the same. As competitive as they are with each other, you'd think they would try to wear distinct clothing and hairstyles to tell them apart. Instead, they look almost like twins.

Mary looks at the fabric in my stepmother's hands. "What is that?"

"Yes," Beth says, eying the material. "It's lovely."

Griselda smirks. "Ella has saved this fabric to make herself a dress. She has also offered some of it to you as trimming for your dresses for the royal ball."

"Royal ball?" Mary's face lights up.

"Yes," My stepmother answers. "The prince is to choose a wife at the event."

"Can you imagine?" Beth stares at the opposite wall with a faraway look as if caught in a daydream. "Me? The next princess?"

Mary elbows her, startling her out of her reverie. "The prince won't want you. He'll choose me."

"No, he won't." Beth snarls. "He'll definitely prefer me. *I'm* the pretty one."

"Take what you need for trim," I interrupt, drawing their attention back to me. "But please make sure to leave me enough to make myself a dress for the ball."

They blink down at me in astonishment.

Mary is the first one down the stairs. She studies the fabric with a scrutinizing gaze. "Where did you get this?"

"I saved it. This is all the scraps left behind from the dressmaker and—"

"Why, you little thief!" Griselda says, and then slaps me again. "I knew this material looked familiar."

I place my hand over my face and stare up at her in fear. "I—I didn't steal it. It was meant to be thrown away. I merely saved it to use later and—"

She slaps me again, this time much harder. Standing to

full height, she glares down at me and points to the wall. "Stand there," she commands.

"But, Stepmother, I—"

"Now," she says in a low voice full of anger.

Hesitantly, I move to the wall and place my palms flat against it as I brace myself for my beating.

"Your dress," she says, reminding me to slip out of the top half to reveal my back.

Shakily, I do as she asks. I cringe as I hear the side table drawer open and slam to a close.

No sooner does my dress fall to my waist than the crack of the lash rips across my skin like fire. Every nerve ending jolts with excruciating pain. I try but fail to suppress a whimper on the second whip. But on the third and fourth, I cry out in agony. She stops after the fifth, and it takes everything I have to remain standing.

She grips my chin and directs my face toward her; I can barely make out her pitying look through my tears. "You know I hate to do that to you, but I have no choice, Ella. I don't want you to grow up a thief, you know."

I lower my eyes as I swallow back a sob and lift my dress, securing it around my shoulders again. "I understand, Stepmother."

A faint smile curves her lips. "Now then. We'll be back later tonight."

With that, she turns and leaves. I note that she takes the fabric with her, passing it off to my stepsisters. They glare at me a moment before leaving as well, taking my glimmer of hope for a better life with them.

Swallowing back a sob, I wipe the moisture from my face and then gather food for Cash and Finn. Everything hurts so badly it's difficult to walk. Holding the wall, it takes all my strength to make it back up the stairs, and when I do, I'm fighting back tears from the pain.

Pushing the door open, my foot snags on the raised entryway, and I trip forward. Hissing, I barely catch myself in time before stumbling to the floor.

Cash and Finn rush toward me, worry etched in their features.

I manage a faint smile at Finn, thankful that he's feeling well enough to stand.

"Ella." He gently smooths the hair back from my face as he stares down at me in concern. "What happened to you?"

He places a hand on my back, and I inhale sharply from the pain.

"What is wrong?" Cash gives me a panicked look. "Why are—"

He stops as he stares down at Finn's hand, stained red with the blood that has seeped through the back of my dress.

Finn's gaze hardens. "Who did this to you?"

I shake my head. "It's all right. I'm used to it."

"Who hurt you, Ella?" Cash demands, his eyes full of fiery rage. "Tell me."

Ashamed, I lower my head, afraid to see their reactions. "My stepmother. But it's all right. I'll be fine."

"Cash, go back to the garden," Finn directs. "I saw some tavan there. We can use it to make a poultice."

When Cash leaves, Finn grabs my hand, ushering me back to the bed where he was lying not long ago himself. As I sit, I think on how strange it is that our roles have reversed so quickly.

His eyes are full of sadness as he kneels beside me. "I need to cleanse your wounds."

"I can do it," I offer. After all, I've had much practice over the past few years having to take care of them myself without aid.

"Please, Ella. Will you allow me to, at least, assess your injuries?"

Normally, I'd be too shy to allow him to touch me. Especially since I've never been touched by any man before. I don't know why, but I instinctively trust Cash and Finn. After all, they jumped in front of me when the wolf came, shielding me from the attack.

I nod, and he carefully unfastens the top half of my dress. He inhales sharply as it falls away from my shoulders, revealing my wounds.

CHAPTER 3

FINN

My heart clenches as I stare down at her back. Blood seeps from her many wounds. But even more disturbing are the crisscross patterns of old scars beneath them, suggesting this is not the first time she's been hurt in this way.

"Ella?" I clench my fists as I try to hold back the rage that I feel toward her stepmother. "How many times has she done this to you?"

She sniffles and looks away, as if ashamed. "It's only when I make her mad. She only does five lashes now. She used to do ten in the beginning, but she knows that takes too long to heal. As it is, I'll be unable to work for the next few days."

"And who takes care of you while you recover?"

She bites her lips and then swallows back a sob. "No one."

Tears sting my eyes as I think about all she has suffered, and I struggle to blink them back. She turns to me and grabs my hand, giving it a gentle squeeze.

"I'm all right, Finn. I've had worse. I'll be fine."

Her blue eyes hold mine, bright with tears, as I place my hand over hers. Despite her pain, she tries to reassure me. She is strong, and I have never admired anyone as much as I do her in this moment. The Elders did indeed choose a worthy female for us to guard. She will make a good queen. "Ella," I breathe her name, barely managing to speak through my sadness. "Please, let me take care of you."

She shakes her head softly. "You don't have to, Finn, I'll—"

"I want to, Ella," I murmur. "Please, allow me to tend you."

After a moment, she nods. I dip a clean cloth in fresh water and drag it gently across her back to cleanse her wounds.

A soft whimper escapes her as I carefully wipe away the blood. The lash marks are deep; I can only imagine how painful this must be for her.

She hugs her knees to her chest as she glances over her shoulder. "Where are you from?"

"Our people make their home deep in the forest. Our kingdom is hidden behind a veil of magic, concealing us from humans."

She looks out the broken window toward the estate's forest. "How many others are there like you?"

A grin tilts my lips. Ella is strong, I observe as she fights back her pain, distracting herself with conversation, and asking questions. "Many."

"How have I never seen one of you before?"

"You probably have," I tease, not wanting to give her all the secrets we keep from humans. She may be our future queen, but it isn't my place to reveal everything to her. "We rarely venture out of the veil, and when we do, humans cannot tell the difference between a normal animal and a shifter." I pause. "And when we are in our human form, we appear as one of your people."

She turns her head and gives me a strange look. "In the

forest... I could hear your voice in my head and that of the wolf. How is that possible?"

"Your father had the gift, did he not?"

Her mouth drifts open, but she quickly snaps it shut and nods.

"We were told that you have it too... that the gift was passed down through his line. When you heard me in the forest, I knew it was true."

A faint smile crests her lips. "All that time..." She shakes her head softly. "I thought my father was telling tales. But now I know he really *was* able to speak to animals."

"Shifters," I correct.

A grin tugs at her mouth. "Shifters," she repeats in agreement.

I continue to cleanse her skin and wonder how much permanent damage will be left behind. I've heard that humans value unmarked skin on their mates, and I wonder if the prince will reject her because of this.

If only we had come sooner, we could've prevented all of the harm that was done to her. Why weren't we sent to gather her as soon as her father died?

"Not all animals are shifters," I continue. "And there are fewer of us now compared to the olden days. It is rare for my kind to reveal themselves to yours, but I know of a few who talked with your father."

Her eyes widen. "Did you know my father?"

I shake my head. "I did not know him personally, but I knew of him."

"And what of my mother? I was so small when she died, I don't remember her well, but was she able to speak with your kind also?"

My heart clenches as her face lights up when she mentions her mother. Life hasn't been fair for our Ella. I feel as if it is our fault for not coming soon enough to protect her from the evils of the world. She had to experience the loss of not one but both of her parents, all by herself.

I think again of the terrible marks on her back. She has been left at the mercy of a vile woman for so many years.

"No. She did not possess the gift. Only those of your father's line have it."

She frowns. "I wonder why that is."

In truth, I know the answer, but it is not my place to tell her. At least, not yet. I should not even have revealed myself to her this soon, but the wolf made my decision for me. As it is, Nyx and Kai are going to have my head. Me *and* Cash. But surely after we tell them why we did this, they'll understand. After all, if it had been Devon with her instead of us, I'm confident he would have done the same.

"Not all have the gift," I offer by way of explanation. "Very few can speak with us in animal form. And even fewer can also communicate with us in our minds while we are in our human forms."

She looks up at me, hope filling her once again. "Am I able to?"

I close my eyes and concentrate, sending her a message. *"Can you hear me?"* I project with my thoughts.

A smile curves her lips, and her eyes sparkle as she grabs my hands. "You're speaking in my mind?"

I nod. *"Of course."*

"That's amazing."

I am glad that I can make the moment lighter for her.

The door jerks open. Ella jumps in shock and winces from the sudden movement. A hiss of pain escapes her as she tries to cover herself up from the intruder.

When she realizes it's Cash, she relaxes.

He drops to his knees beside me. "Here," he says, handing me the small bowl of tavan. "I've already made it into a poultice."

Relief floods me that we can finally relieve her pain. Scooping some of the mixture, I look down at Ella. "This should help you heal faster, and it will take away your pain."

"Thank you."

Cash tenderly brushes her hair forward over her shoulder so I can apply the medicine.

As I smooth the poultice over her injuries, a small sigh escapes her. I watch in satisfaction as her entire body slowly begins to relax even more. When I finish, I find another cloth and carefully cover her back. With the poultice, her wounds should be closed entirely by tomorrow evening. "I must bind this around you, all right?" I ask because it means I might see her exposed front.

Judging from the deep crimson coloring of her cheeks earlier, she seems rather shy about nudity. But then again, I've heard that most humans are.

"I understand."

At first, she covers her breasts with her hands. A pink flush creeps up her neck to her cheeks.

"We will not hurt you," I say, trying to reassure her we will not take advantage of her in this state. It is something we would never do.

She nods and lowers her gaze. Her cheeks bloom a deeper shade of red as she replies, "I trust you."

Ella closes her eyes and then lifts her arms so I can begin wrapping the cloth around her. As she leans forward, the back of my hand brushes across her breast. The soft pink nipple turns into a hard bead at the contact, and she gasps.

"Forgive me," I tell her, ashamed. The last thing I want her to think is that I am behaving inappropriately. I am her guard. I would never take advantage of her, but she does not know this.

My nostrils flare as her delicate scent grows stronger, and my brother looks to me, communicating with his thoughts. *"She is attracted to us,"* his voice whispers in my mind in wonder.

"How do you know?" I project my question to him, refusing to allow myself to become hopeful.

"Her scent. It is stronger now."

"Attracted to us?" I ask. *"Or simply to me?"* I tease him.

He narrows his eyes at me but tips his head as if considering. *"It is not unheard of for a female to mate one of her guards. It is unusual,"* he adds. *"But it has happened before."*

My heart stops and the begins pounding. This beautiful female is attracted to me? Surely not. After all, I am not as handsome as Nyx or Kai. Once she sees them, she will surely forget me. Me *and* Cash, I think to myself.

Which reminds me: *"When are the others coming?"*

"Not until tomorrow."

I'm not ashamed to admit that this makes me somewhat happy. I miss my bond brothers, but I am glad Cash and I will be able to spend more time with her by ourselves until they arrive.

Having sensed my thoughts, he arches a brow at me. *"It is her destiny to marry the prince. We are her guards, and that is all we can ever be to her. Do you understand?"*

Reluctantly, I nod.

"Once the others are here, they will explain everything to her," he adds, and my mood turns sour. I'm not sure how she'll take this news. She only just learned of our world. If her father had lived, she would have been introduced to it earlier, but because he did not... there is no way to ease her into it. We'll just have to hope she does not have trouble accepting us as her guards and the truth of the prophecy.

At least it seems that she already trusts us to keep her safe. She must already be feeling the instinctual pull of a female to her guards. It is not uncommon for the bonds of trust to forge so quickly.

Ella's eyes grow heavy-lidded once I finish, and she lies down on her side. "You can sleep, Ella. We will take care of you."

She gives me a faint smile. "Thank you, Finn. Thank you, Cash." She yawns. "I'm so glad I met you. I would have been dead if—"

Cash puts a finger softly to her lips. "Shhh. Do not think on it, Ella," he murmurs. "You are safe now. We will protect you."

He looks at me and stands. "I am going downstairs to secure the tower. I will return shortly."

I nod in acknowledgment and turn my attention back to Ella.

"You can lie down if you want," she whispers, as her cheeks redden yet again.

I'm definitely not going to argue or protest. I can think of nothing I want more than to lie next to Ella and bathe myself in her scent. I've heard that the bond between a female and her guards is strong, but I thought it would not be so until after she sealed it. It seems I was wrong.

Something dark and primal stirs within me as I stare down at her smaller form. I would live for her; I would die for her. I would sacrifice everything. And I feel as if I'm the happiest of males simply *because* I am hers. Has a guard ever been paired with a more perfect female?

I think not.

I clench my jaw in frustration, for I understand what is already happening. It is known as the great temptation, according to the Elders who trained us. To be so intimately linked to a female, as her guard, is to bind one's soul to hers.

The Elders warned each of us: me, Cash, Nyx, Kai, and Devon. They told us we would be tempted to claim her as ours but that such a thing could never be. She is the Chosen One—the one foretold of in the ancient prophecy. She is fated to marry the prince. To unite our two kingdoms as they used to be before the great war and the divide that followed.

My father told Cash and me that we were blessed to be chosen as her guards, but I did not understand at the time. I stare down at her delicate form as she sleeps. She is completely captivating with her silken golden hair spread out on the pillow beneath her, long lashes fanned across soft pink cheeks, and her perfect lips partially open in a small *o*.

Yes, I would gladly sacrifice my life for Ella.

I lie beside her. Allowing me to lie this close to her so soon... she must feel the pull of the bond, even if she does not recognize it for what it is. Instinctively, she moves closer to me as if seeking warmth and protection. Unable to resist, I carefully drape my arm over her and hold her closer against my chest.

Her eyelids flutter and open. A pink bloom spreads across her cheeks. "I don't normally sleep with strange men."

Something about her words fills me with a fierce possessiveness.

She is mine to guard and protect. I would never allow another male this close to her—besides my bond brothers, of course. My thoughts turn to the prince, but I force myself to focus on something else, refusing to think about how she is fated to be his. I don't want to ruin this perfect moment by imagining her in his arms as his mate.

"Is this all right?" The last thing I want to do is cause her any discomfort.

She smiles again, and I am completely enchanted. "Yes," she breathes. "I... I trust you. And Cash. I don't know how to explain it." She reaches across and touches my cheek as her blue eyes search mine in wonder. "Even though we just met, I feel... connected to you somehow. Does that make sense?"

Unable to help myself, I lean forward and place a soft kiss on her forehead. "I feel the same. And the more time we spend together, the stronger our bond as your guards will become. Soon, you may even be able to sense our thought speech without even having to try. It will simply come naturally." I pause. "At least… that is how it is with a shifter female and her guards. So, I believe it will be the same for you as well."

She softly bites her lower lip. I reach out and brush her hair back from her face. "We will take care of you, Ella. You are safe with us. My vow."

I'm pleased when she nestles against me closing her eyes.

I hold her close, relishing the feel of her in my arms.

When Cash returns, he lies down behind her. His gaze searches mine a moment, as if asking permission. We share everything, he and I. We always have since we were young, but it is different with Ella. Never once did either of us imagine sharing a closeness like this with the same female.

We knew as her guards we would protect her, but I can see in his eyes that, like me, he did not realize how strong this pull to her would become. I can sense his deep longing to hold her close, for his desire echoes my own. I nod, and he moves closer to her, draping his arm across her as well.

She releases a soft sigh of contentment between us, and my heart fills with happiness at the knowledge that she already feels so comfortable with us both. This is good. Perhaps she will accept the rest of her guards as quickly as she seems to have accepted us.

The sooner, the better, for danger is coming.

That wolf shifter was only the first. Soon, I suspect there will be more. She will need all of us to protect her when that happens. For not all wish to see the prophecy come to pass. They see Ella as a threat and will do anything to keep her from her destiny.

The prophecy states that the Chosen One will possess the ability to speak to our kind through the mind speech, as she has already done. It also states that she will have the power to heal the land. This will be the proof that she is the one foretold in the ancient texts.

The Elders do not know what form her power will take. They only know that as it grows stronger, people will be drawn to the inner light of her magic, even if they do not recognize it for what it is.

That must be how the wolf shifter knew where she was. He was able to sense her power. After all, it is how Cash and I located her. Her inner light is so strong that the moment we crossed the veil we were immediately drawn to the forest behind the estate. When we saw her in the clearing, we knew immediately that she was the one we'd been sent to guard.

I think on the land surrounding the estate. It is green and full of life whereas all else beyond it is dry and nearly barren. On our journey here I noticed several fields full of withering crops. I wonder how long it has been this way in the human kingdom?

In ours, only the past few years have been hard. Our leader—the wolf queen—has reassured us that all will be well. But rain is such a rare thing nowadays, many have begun to lose hope.

My own family is struggling to survive on the meager harvest they gathered last fall. As my gaze drifts to Ella, I understand how important is our mission as her guards. She is destined to unite our two kingdoms and bring healing to our people and to our lands.

Gently, I tug her closer to my chest. I clench my jaw as guilt moves through me. I wish I could tell her everything, but it is not my place. So much responsibility already rests on her shoulders and she does not even know it yet.

CHAPTER 4

CASH

We switch places during the night so Finn can take a turn going downstairs to check for any danger. I do not think anyone would dare try to attack us now, especially since two of us watch over her, but we cannot be certain.

She must be kept safe at all costs.

Soft light from a small candle in the corner of the room illuminates her features. She is the most beautiful female I have ever beheld. As if knowing I wish to study her luminous blue eyes, her eyelids flutter and open. "Where is Finn going?" she asks. I'm surprised that she can tell us apart. Even my bond brothers often have trouble doing this.

I tuck a stray tendril of hair behind her ear, the silken strands soft beneath my fingers. "We are taking turns guarding downstairs."

She stiffens in my arms, and the acrid scent of her fear fills my nostrils. "You think someone might come after me here?

I hate that my words have caused her to be afraid, so I quickly move to reassure her. "All is well. We are just being safe. I doubt any would try to harm you with two of us here."

She gives me a strange look. "Why me? What's so special about me? Is it because I can communicate with your kind in my thoughts?"

I want so much to tell her everything, but I know I should wait for the rest of our bond brothers to arrive. So, for now I will give her a simple answer. "Yes."

She lowers her gaze. A small crease of worry forms across her brow.

I reach out and gently smooth my thumb over it, as if to ease her concern. "You do not need to be afraid, Ella. Finn and I will protect you."

She gives me a faint smile. "I trust you."

My heart feels full. She has been through much, this female. And for her to trust us is a precious gift. One I vow I will never abuse. I press a soft kiss to her cheek, then smile at the pink flush left behind in its wake. She is precious, our Ella. "We will protect you," I swear. "My vow."

She nods, closes her eyes, and then goes back to sleep. It is an effect of the poultice that she is able to drift away so easily. Its ability to soothe pain also causes drowsiness. I am glad she is able to rest despite her injuries.

When Finn returns, I am loath to trade places with him again, but I do. I wish to spend as much time holding her as I can. Once she mates the prince, I will only be able to guard her from afar.

Human males are not known to share their mates like shifters often do. The Elders explained it has something to do with possession and passing their property to their heirs. They want the assurance that a child born of their female is of their seed and no others.

Whereas shifters, we prefer safety in numbers. When we

choose to become part of a harem and share a female, it means that any offspring she has will be accepted by each male. They will always have protection and be well provided for.

With a heavy sigh, I carefully untangle myself from her arms and watch as my brother takes my place. It is difficult to push down my jealousy, but I somehow manage.

This is the first time I've ever been jealous of Finn. As far as I can remember, we've always shared everything. But this? This is different. I want her all to myself.

Even though my kind are known to form harems, it is not unheard of for males to experience some tension amongst each other, fighting for the attention of their female and vying to become her favorite.

During our training, the Elders tried to prepare us for the intense possessiveness we would likely experience toward the female we would guard. They warned us of the strong pull of the bond, informing us that it would only grow stronger once she sealed us to her permanently.

The bond between female and guard is cemented with a kiss. But this is how it is done among shifters. Ella is human, and I wonder if the bond can be sealed in this way.

I sigh heavily as I try to push down the fierce possession deep inside me as I hold her. It is easy to see that my brother struggles with this too. I know we're not the first to feel this way, and we certainly won't be the last. I should be grateful we have this time with her alone... before everyone else arrives and before she fulfills her destiny and marries the prince.

CHAPTER 5

DEVON

We are on our way to find the Chosen One—she whom we will guard. As we make our way through the woods, we decide to travel along the river. I detest being so close to the water, but Kai insisted we come this way. He is right, I suppose. If an enemy tracks us, it is easier to lose them by crossing the water frequently so they cannot follow our scent.

The normally silken black fur of my feline form is still wet from our last crossing. I look up at Kai. His blue feathers gleam brightly beneath the sun as he flies overhead. What does he care about water? He is not the one who has to get wet, I think bitterly. But still, he is our leader, and we must do as he says.

Nyx appears just as miserable as I am. His light brown fur sodden and clinging to his rabbit form. He casts a sideways glance at me. *"What are you looking at?"* he projects.

Of all of us, he is the one I have the most difficult time getting along with. I suppose it is the nature of what we are.

The Elders, at first, were hesitant to place us in the same bond brother group, even though we each possessed the Mark of the Chosen. Rabbits and cats are archenemies in our world. But after seeing our strengths and knowing that the one we'd be protecting was so important, they bonded us after all.

They were hesitant to bond me and Kai as brothers as well since he is a blue jay. Truth be told, cat shifters have many in our kingdom we do not get along with. I think the Elders recognized this and that is how they decided to approve our brother bonds with each other.

How could they not? The prophecy foretold our bonding, and we were each recognized from birth because of our marks. I care for my rabbit bond brother. He is just difficult sometimes, and I love to tease him. My lips tilt up in a grin. *"You look terrible, Nyx."*

Nyx narrows his brown eyes and kicks out at me, sending me flying into the river. The freezing water takes my breath away as soon as I hit the surface. My tired limbs refuse to move as quickly as I want as I struggle to swim against the current. It takes all my strength to keep my head above water, and when I climb up to the bank, I hiss and growl my displeasure as I shake off my paws. *"What was that for, you insufferable rabbit?"*

"Who looks terrible now, Devon?" He smirks.

I lift my paw to swipe at him, but Kai darts down and lights in front of me. He gives us each a stern look. His blue eyes blazing with anger. *"Stop it, you two. You need to get along. It will not look good to be fighting in front of our female when we reach her. We must appear to be united."*

Nyx purses his lips. *"We are, Kai."*

"Yes," I agree, smirking as I eye Nyx with the promise of revenge. *"We were just having a bit of fun. Weren't we, Nyx?"*

In this, we are a team. We hate being scolded by our

leader and try to pass off our fighting as friendly play, even if it isn't always so.

"*Yes*," Nyx clips.

Kai narrows his eyes and nods before taking to the air once more. "*Let us hurry then. We're almost there.*"

Drawn to our brothers, Cash and Finn, it does not take long to locate them using the bond between us. We are still not in range to speak in their minds, but I know they are close.

"*There.*" I point ahead to the large estate in the distance.

It is a well-known landmark among our kind for it sits at the edge of the forest, near our kingdom. Everyone knows that in it resides the descendant of the line that can speak to our kind in animal form—she who was foretold in the ancient prophecy. Ella: The Chosen One.

The entire structure is palatial. Nearly rivaling the size of a castle. It seems our female is one that lives in comfort. I wonder if she will be like the royalty of our world: pampered and selfish. Hopefully not, but even if she is, it will be our duty to see she is well, comfortable, protected, and safe.

I study the building. Four levels full of floor to ceiling windows look out onto a large garden of trees and various flowering plants. Bright blooms of blues, yellows, and reds fill the entire space. Vines wind up a trellis continuing up the side of the main house, blanketing it in a beautiful carpet of green. Despite its beauty, the structure was certainly not built for any defense, and I wonder how we can fortify it a bit more in case of attack.

There are rumors that some of our kind want to kill the Chosen One to prevent the prophecy from being fulfilled. There are even rumblings that the Wolf Queen is among them.

Many shifters detest the humans completely. They're angered at the mere thought of our kingdoms uniting once more as they were in the days of old because they do not trust the humans. Too much blood was spilled between us before the Elders finally erected the magical Veil, concealing our kingdom from them to keep our people safe from being hunted.

Humans hunted and killed shifters in droves only a few generations ago, before we convinced their kind that we were simply myths and legends. The veiled barrier of magic between our two kingdoms has protected us since then, but our people have long lives, and many still harbor anger toward humans.

It is forbidden to take a human through the Veil, and we are warned from the time we are children that it is not wise to live among the humans. Yet, many still do, hiding what they are by making sure never to shift into their animal forms. As I think on all the stories I heard as a child of humans killing our kind, I can hardly believe that some shifters take this risk and make their homes and livelihoods in the human world.

My father says that when I was born, my mother cried herself to sleep for many nights, lamenting that the mark was upon my skin. It designated me as a guard of the Chosen One and meant that I would have to one day go to the human world.

Closing my eyes, I think back on her tears as I left with my bond brothers to cross the Veil. She does not believe I will ever make it back home again, despite all my assurances.

"Devon?" Kai whispers, snapping me back from my troubled thoughts. "What do you think?"

I allow my gaze to travel over the entire estate. A tall tower on one side is where I feel pulled to the strongest, and I stare at it curiously. I wonder why our female would choose to be up there. In comparison to the main house, this appears a bit run down. As if it has fallen into a state of disrepair from the rest of the immaculately kept structure.

As we make our way cautiously through the garden, I note all the vegetables that appear to be growing here. It's strange how everything here seems to be flourishing while the area around the estate looks so dry; even much of the fields and grass are brown.

There is a great myth among our people about the Chosen One's family line. It is said that her ancestor saved the life of one of the shifter queens of old. In thanks for saving her, the queen blessed them with the gift of magic. She also gave them the ability to understand our mind speech. This ability was then passed down to their ancestors.

The prophecy states that the Chosen One will possess the ability to speak to our kind in her mind and the power to heal the land. The Elders believe she may have inherited the magic that was bestowed upon her ancestor by the ancient queen. Seeing how prosperous the estate's grounds are, compared to everywhere else, I think there may be truth to this story. The land here appears healthier, more vibrant, and green than it does throughout the rest of the kingdom.

But the Elders are uncertain what type of power she possesses to heal the land in such a way, believing it may be mastery of one of the elements. They only know for certain that as it grows stronger, so does her inner light. Many will be drawn to it, able to recognize her for who and what she is.

This includes her enemies—the ones who do not want peace with the humans and the ones who believe that the Chosen One is an abomination. Many shifters study magic in various forms, but it is rare for any of them to be able to influence the elements in any way. So, many of my kind think it wrong for a human to possess the power of magic— especially that of the elements.

When we step through the tower door from the garden, I

lift my gaze to the spiraling wooden staircase above us. A cold draft blows through the space, and I shiver slightly. Why on earth would she choose a place like this when the rest of the house is so grand?

I turn to find Nyx and Kai studying the structure, and I don't have to read their minds to know that they're thinking the same thing. Nyx turns to me in confusion. *"Why this place?"*

"Yes," Kai adds. *"I was wondering the same thing."*

I shrug. *"I suppose we'll find out. First, let's find Cash and Finn. Maybe they can fill us in. After all, they've been watching over her since yesterday."*

Quietly, Nyx and I ascend the staircase. Kai does not have to take as much care since he can simply fly alongside us. Sometimes I envy him his ability to fly, but then again, I do feel that my form is superior in many ways. For instance, I dart a glance at Nyx, clumsily making his way up the stairs. It is much easier to move with stealth in a cat form versus that of a rabbit.

He narrows his eyes at me. *"Why do I feel like you're judging me?"*

A sly grin crests my lips. *"I would never..."*

He rolls his eyes and shifts.

Kai swirls around and gapes at him. *"What are you doing?"*

Nyx stands before him, unapologetically, in his human form. He rakes a hand through his short chestnut hair as his brown eyes meet Kai's evenly. *"I cannot move as quietly as a rabbit up those steps. This way is much easier."*

"But she might see you and get scared," Kai projects so loudly in my thoughts it's as if my brain is ringing with alarms.

"If I hear any indication of someone approaching, I'll shift back," he reassures Kai.

Kai says nothing, so feeling rebellious, I shift as well.

Kai spins back. *"You too?"* he asks accusingly.

I comb my fingers through my still damp black hair, smoothing it back from my forehead before I gesture to my bond brother. *"If Nyx can, why can't I?"*

Kai sighs heavily and shifts as well. His golden hair reflects the soft moonlight that spills in through a broken window as his sharp blue eyes meet ours.

I arch a brow, and he shrugs. *"We'll just have to shift back quickly if we hear anyone approach."*

It feels like forever before we reach the top of the stairs. When we do, a small light under the door gives us pause.

Cautiously, since I am the one with cat's feet, I quietly move to the opening and carefully push it back just enough to peer inside.

My jaw drops when I see Cash and Finn both in human form with a female between them. I blink several times in shock before spinning back to Kai and Nyx.

"What is it?" Kai asks.

"Yes, what did you see?" Nyx's brown eyes search mine.

I struggle to come up with an answer, something that will not get my bond brothers in trouble.

Despite his charming and normally easy-going nature, Kai can be a stern leader. He demands that we obey the decisions he makes for our group. We chose him because he is wise and we all respect him.

Cash and Finn have always been rather impulsive and prone to mischief, but I'm shocked that they blatantly disregarded Kai's order that we not reveal our human forms to our female yet. Kai will be furious if he sees them like this.

I cannot send them a thought communication, warning them we are here, without risking that Kai and Nyx would pick up on it as well. What on earth would possess them to be sleeping in human form with the female we're only supposed to be guarding from the shadows?

Kai pushes past me, and I grab his arm. *"Don't!"*

His blue eyes snap to me. *"What are you doing? What's going on? Why are you acting so strange?"*

"Just... give it a minute," I tell him.

"Why?"

I push the door, hoping the small creak will alert Cash and Finn so they can change forms before Kai and Nyx see them.

"She's unclothed," I explain, cringing from my poor excuse. *"And you know how humans are about nudity. It is rude to look upon them in such a bare state."*

Kai frowns but then nods and stays where he is. I notice Nyx, however, carefully edging closer to the opening, trying to look inside.

"Stop!" I tell him. *"What are you doing?"*

He narrows his eyes. *"You are stalling."*

"No, I am not," I snap.

"Yes, you are. I know you. Besides, if she is unclothed, why should it matter?" he says as he tries to pass me. *"It's not as if nudity is wrong."*

"It is for humans," I glare at him. *"You know it's true. We aren't in a shifter village anymore. Humans are always fully clothed."*

Crossing his arms over his chest, he purses his lips. *"Fine. We will wait a moment for her to dress."*

Nyx is second in command behind Kai. When we were deciding who would lead us, he was the only other consideration. Kai was ultimately chosen because of his innate ability to put others at ease. He is charismatic and able to get along with almost anyone.

Whereas, Nyx tends to be stern and unmovable. When he decides upon something there is very little that can change his mind once it's made up. He respects Kai and they are very close, but he often dislikes being told what to do. Especially by me.

And now that we're so close to the Chosen One—she whom we have trained our entire lives to protect, Nyx is impatient to see her. I don't know how long I'll be able to stall him.

I know he has dreamed of her many times, but he is hesitant when he speaks of it. We've been bond brothers long enough that I know when Nyx does not discuss the details of his dreams, it is for one of two reasons: Either he has had a vision of the future, or a warning.

He was more agitated than usual on our journey here today, and I believe it was because he knew we were finally going to see her. I only hope that whatever Nyx saw of her in his dreams, that it was something favorable and not terrible.

After a few moments, I peek inside the door once more, and both Cash and Finn lift their heads. Their green eyes meet mine as I try to mouth the word "shift" to them.

The two idiots remain where they are, ignoring my attempt to spare them from Kai's anger.

I roll my eyes and shake my head in frustration. I was trying to save them from Kai's wrath.

Having waited long enough, Kai pushes past me to step in. He stops, and his jaw drops when he sees them. *"What are you doing?"* he yells through the bond.

"Ella wanted us to sleep with her like this," they both answer quickly.

"She what?" he asks, still staring at them in shock.

Nyx walks in, a stunned look on his face as well.

Carefully, Cash unwraps his arm from around the female and walks toward us. Finn, however, stays where he is. And I'm not sure if it's my imagination, but it looks as though he pulled her possessively closer to him.

"Explain yourself, right now," Kai demands.

With a heavy sigh, Cash rakes a hand through his light brown hair and then launches into a long explanation starting with an attack in the woods. When he tells us he killed a wolf shifter, Nyx gasps. *"They already sent one after her?"* he asks, alarm easily read in his features.

Cash frowns and then nods.

Stunned by Nyx's question, I look to him. *"You expected that to happen?"*

I'm even more surprised when he, Cash, and Finn nod. It seems my bond brother confided in them and not me.

"I dreamed of it," Nyx answers. *"I dreamed that the Wolf Queen herself was coming to kill the Chosen One."*

I glare at him accusingly. *"You intentionally withheld this from me and—"* I'm about to say "Kai," but as I look to our leader, I realize he does not appear surprised either. It seems I am the only one Nyx did not share his dream with. I snap my jaw shut. I should be used to this. I'm always considered the outsider among my bond brothers. Even among shifters, cats are outcasts.

"I thought it would not happen until after her marriage to the prince," Nyx adds. *"Otherwise, I would have insisted we all come sooner."*

Kai turns to Cash. *"Well then, it seems as though you did not have a choice. But what have you told her?"*

"Nothing," Finn answers from across the room, his green eyes practically burning into ours. I've never seen him appear as possessive over something as he appears to be with our female.

"You told her nothing?" Nyx asks incredulously. *"But you said she saw you shift."*

"She did. And she accepts that we are shifters here to protect her," Cash adds. *"Saving her from that wolf shifter was fate, for it made her more willing to accept us for who we are."*

"I believe she feels the pull of the bond but does not realize what it is yet," Finn explains as he tenderly brushes a stray tendril of hair behind her ear. *"Because she already trusts us complete-*

ly." He gestures to her smaller form, snuggled against him, and unbidden jealousy flares to life deep inside me.

Where on earth did that come from? I should not be feeling this way. Especially not toward a human—the female we are supposed to guard.

Quietly, we approach and stare down at our female. The one we have trained for so many years to protect.

The mark on my arm begins to burn slightly. It's not painful, but it's enough to get my attention. I glance down at my forearm and notice the rest of my bond brothers doing the same. The small whirling pattern on our skin glows softly, and when I lift my gaze, we all stare at each other a moment before looking back down at her.

This is confirmation that she is indeed the one. The Elders told us that our marks would alert us when we'd found the Chosen One that we were bound to protect with our lives.

She has not even sealed us to her as guards, but already we respond to her as if we are.

With long, blonde hair, pink cheeks, and full lips, her form is so slight; she is both delicate and beautiful in the same measure. The soft light of the lone candle lends her an ethereal glow. I am captivated and completely enchanted. Is this what it feels like to lose one's heart to a female?

I've heard of females mating to one of their guards. It is rare, but it has happened before. But it cannot be this way for us. It is our duty to make sure she weds the prince of this kingdom. It is her fate to restore the balance between our two worlds. She will be the bridge between shifters and humans.

Once peace is restored, our people can stop living in fear of being hunted. All can be as it was in the time of my great-grandparents, when shifters and humans lived among one another without conflict.

Even as this thought churns through my mind, I find myself overcome with jealousy as I look at Finn. A soft sigh escapes her lips, and she snuggles even closer to his chest.

Fierce possessiveness fills me as my gaze travels over her form. I level an angry glare at the mischievous twins. Their animal form matches their human personality—always getting into trouble and always getting away with it. They should not be sleeping so close to her.

Quietly, I slip into the bed behind her.

"What are you doing?" Finn snaps, jealousy lacing his voice.

I arch a brow. *"I'm merely keeping her warm."* If they can sleep next to her, so can I.

"You're going to scare her," Cash says. *"She does not know you yet."*

I ignore him as I lay down beside her and close my eyes. My nostrils flare as I drink in her delicate scent. She smells delicious, and she feels so warm. My arm fits nicely around her smaller form, and as I lightly tug her back against me and away from my bond brother Finn, I marvel at how she seems to mold against me like this, as if made for me. I cannot help the low rumbling purr that begins deep in my chest. My tail comes out as I partially shift, wrapping itself around her ankle.

Cats are naturally warmer than most creatures. She seems to sense this because she presses herself back against me. I long to bury my nose in her hair, but I refrain. She is not my mate; I am merely providing her warmth. A duty that any guard would do for their female.

Something tugs at my shoulder, and my eyes snap open to find Nyx. It figures the annoying rabbit would try to pull me away, probably because he wants to take my place.

Kai's expression is thunderous as he stares down at me. "Get up," he says in a harsh whisper, not bothering to use the mind link anymore. "Now."

I look across at Finn and gesture. "What about him? Aren't you going to tell him anything?"

Kai grits his teeth.

I sigh heavily, not wanting to follow our leader's order. "Fine."

I start to get up, but Ella turns to face me. I'm so panicked, I shift, and so does everyone else, except for Cash and Finn.

She blinks several times in confusion and sits up. She looks at Cash. "What's going on?"

He gives her a nervous grin. "The rest of our bond brothers are here."

"Bond... brothers?" She scrunches her face in confusion.

He gestures to each of us. Ella leans forward, wincing as she does so, and I panic, shifting back into a human. Something stirs deep inside me, wanting desperately to soothe whatever has pained her. "What is wrong?"

She shrieks and scrambles back into Finn's arms. "Who are you?"

"Conjure some clothes for your human form," Finn snaps, pointing to my manhood in disapproval. "She is human. They do not like nudity, remember?"

Her eyes are wide as they stare down at my cock, and my cheeks burn with embarrassment as I quickly shift so that it appears as if I'm wearing pants like Finn and Cash are.

I hold my hand out to her, palms up. "Forgive me, Ella. I did not mean to scare you. My name is Devon. I am a bond brother to Cash and Finn."

Instantly, she calms as if she trusts me already. "Oh. You're brothers?" I know she probably believes we were born to the same parents, and I do not move to correct her. Not yet, anyway. We can always discuss it later.

"Yes."

Kai and Nyx shift beside me, each of them appearing to

wear pants. I clench my jaw. Why did I not think of that as well before I changed into my human form?

"I am Kai." He bows low in an elegant gesture and smiles up at her, his bright blue eyes practically sparkling with joy as he studies her lovely face.

"And I am Nyx. We are all bond brothers to each other."

She gives us each a dazzling smile that rivals the brightness of the sun. "It is so nice to meet you. I didn't know Cash and Finn even had any other brothers."

Kai arches a brow at them, and they grin sheepishly.

"Did you come because you were worried about them?" she asks. "They're fearless. They saved me yesterday from a wolf shifter. They took care of me after my stepmother..." her voice trails off.

"Beat her," Finn says in a low voice laced with quiet anger.

"Your stepmother beat you?" Nyx kneels beside her as his fists clench by his side. "Why?"

Ella lowers her head. "She thought I was stealing."

Kai blinks down at her and shakes his head in confusion. "Stealing?"

"I had saved up material that was discarded by the dressmaker when he came to fit my sisters." She sniffs. "It would have just been thrown away if I hadn't saved it."

Kai cups her chin, lifting her face to meet his. Her eyes are bright with tears, and my heart clenches as the first one escapes her lashes and rolls gently down her cheek. He brushes it away with the soft pad of his thumb. "You did nothing wrong." He speaks in a quiet tone. "You are not a thief."

"Thank you."

CHAPTER 6

KAI

My heart squeezes painfully in my chest at her tears. What cruel twist of fate left her at the hands of such a monster as this stepmother of hers? This woman will pay. My vow.

When I search the eyes of my brothers, it seems we are all in agreement. How dare someone mistreat our female. We are her guards, sworn to defend and protect her, and we will not allow such a transgression to go unpunished.

A cold breeze blows through the broken window of her room, and Ella shivers slightly. This looks more like attic storage than a proper bedroom. Devon picks up old boxes and nearby crates to try and block it as Finn wraps his arms around her. I am not too proud to admit that I am jealous of them or how she snuggles back into the twin. I should not think this way, but I cannot help it. Instinctively, I feel drawn to her, possessive even.

She is such a lovely and delicate creature. Even with her hair slightly disheveled from sleep, she is stunningly beautiful with long lashes and luminous blue eyes that seem to stare straight through me. I am completely captivated. I've heard this can happen to a guard, but I never thought it would happen to me.

How am I going to stand it if we are successful in our mission? How will I be able to stand by and watch her become a mate to the prince? It will be torture to be so often in her presence and never allowed to touch her... to never be able to love her as more than...

I close my eyes and shake my head to clear away my errant thoughts. It is our duty to make certain she weds the prince of this kingdom to restore the balance between our people and the humans. And yet, as I watch her, I would give up everything. Forsake all my training and the vows I swore to uphold if she would agree to become my mate.

Her eyes search mine, and I can think only of the sea. The deep blue of their coloring reminding me of its depths. "Do you know why we are here, Ella?"

Her small brow furrows softly. "No."

"We are your guards, sworn to protect and defend you."

"Defend me against what?"

I dart a glance at Finn and give him a subtle nod to explain. It is easy to see she has complete trust in him and Cash already, so I'd like her to hear this from him.

Understanding what I want him to do, Finn begins. "You are the one foretold, Ella. The Chosen One who will restore peace between our people and yours."

She blinks up at him. "How am I supposed to do that?"

"You are destined to become the mate to the prince of this kingdom. Through your marriage to him, you can be the bridge between our two worlds."

Her eyes search Finn's. "I don't understand. Why me?"

I take her hand, drawing her attention back to me. "You are special, Ella. Your family descends from one who was able to speak to our kind through the mind speech. That is why your father's line has always been able to understand and recognize our kind in our animal form."

A small smile crests her lips. "It's nice to know that my father was telling the truth all that time when he told me he could speak with animals. But... why could I not do it then as well?"

I shake my head softly. "The gift does not manifest until your eighteenth birthday."

She tips her chin up to look back at Finn, who is still holding her. She gives him a dazzling smile, and jealousy spikes through me once again. "That's why you came to me in the woods, isn't it?"

He smiles back at her. "Yes, my Ella."

My eyes snap up to him. *"Your Ella?"*

Even as he tugs her closer into his chest, he at least has the decency to appear chagrined by my question.

I'm shocked when she blinks at me and speaks in my mind. *"Please, do not chastise Finn. He saved me. Besides, I don't mind. I have not been anyone's since my parents died."*

At first, I'm stunned that she even heard me and was able to respond in kind. Is the bond already that strong? Even as I consider this, her words give me pause. We are not supposed to attach ourselves to her in this way. It is our duty to guard her, protect her, defend her, and help her marry the prince. That is all.

I tilt my head to the side to regard her. "Ella, do you feel a... pull to us in any way?"

"Yes." She looks back again at Finn. "I was just talking about this with Finn and Cash. It's strange, but I do feel a connection to them. And actually..." Her gaze travels over me, Nyx, and Devon. "To you as well." She pauses. "It's as if I know you all care about me. That you would never hurt me."

"That is right." I nod encouragingly. "It is part of the bond —the one that forms between a female and her guards."

Cash takes her hand. "We are your guards, Ella."

"But why do I need guards?"

Finn wraps his arms even tighter around her, and she turns to look up at him. "Because of the wolf that came for you in the forest. There may be others."

"Why?" She looks to him in confusion. "What have I done to make them hunt me?"

I know it's irrational since she can never be my mate, but I want her attention on me and not Finn anyway. So, I take her hand gently in mine. "In our kingdom, there are many factions. One of which does not want the reunification of our people with humans. They know that the Elders foretold your coming and what you would do. So, they seek to stop you any way that they can."

She shivers, and I hate the fear in her eyes, especially since my words are the ones that put it there in the first place.

Kneeling before her bed, I lift her hand and press a soft kiss to the back of it. "We will keep you safe, Ella. My vow. No one will be able to harm you now that we are here."

"He's right." Cash steps beside me and grips my shoulder. "We have trained our entire lives to protect you."

"You have?"

"Yes. We are bound to you."

She tips her head to the side to regard me. "Tell me more about this bond."

"All guards have a bond to the one they protect as well as to each other." I close my eyes briefly as I feel of it deep inside me. "Even now, I can feel it strengthening between us. Can you?"

She nods. "In my heart, I know you will never harm me. You will always protect me, and I am safe with all of you.

Even though we just met, it feels as if I have known you my entire life."

I smile. "Yes. That is the bond. And when you have decided that you approve of each of us, you may seal us to you permanently."

Her small brow furrows softly. "How?"

"A kiss."

Her eyes widen slightly as she blushes. "But I've never—"

I move to reassure her. "It is all right, Ella. You do not have to decide upon this yet. You may wish to wait until after you have met the prince." Sadness fills me at the thought of him even touching her; knowing she can never be mine.

"But how will I catch the eye of the prince?" She frowns and waves a hand over her body. "He isn't going to want me looking like this."

I cock my head to the side to regard her. Does she not know she is perfect? She is the most beautiful and enchanting woman my eyes have ever beheld.

"The royal ball," I reply, rubbing my thumb over the back of her hand and reveling in the feel of her soft skin against my own. "There are a few shifters that work in the palace. They are the ones responsible for organizing this event, having planted the idea in the queen's mind."

It is true. The Elders have many agents working toward this end, trying to fulfill the prophecy so that we will once again have peace and unity between our two kingdoms.

Ella frowns as her blue eyes dim even further. "I do not even have a dress for the royal ball."

To my surprise, Devon steps forward. His vertically slit pupils contract and then expand as his green eyes stare down at her, full of devotion. "Leave that to us. You need not worry about anything now that we are here."

CHAPTER 7

NYX

"So, are you the rabbit?" She smiles at me, and my heart stops and then begins pounding against my ribs.

Normally, I am the stoic one and not easily flustered. But when she asks me my name again, all words escape me, including the ability to form any coherent thoughts. All I can think is that she is the most beautiful female I have ever seen.

I have dreamed of her many times, and she is everything I imagined and much more. And I am certain this is not the bond making me feel this way. As her blue eyes stare up at me, I am completely lost. Would that she could be mine. I would treasure her always.

"Nyx." Kai chuckles beside me. His blue eyes dance with barely restrained amusement as he playfully punches at my arm. "Yes he is, and it seems that you"—he arches a brow at her—"are the one and only person capable of rendering him speechless."

Growling, I snap my head toward Kai and narrow my

eyes. That insufferable blue jay. He enjoys watching me flounder like this.

A small snicker off to the side catches my attention, and I notice Devon. His green cat eyes watching me with a sly smirk on his lips.

I clench my jaw in frustration at my inability to compose myself around a beautiful female, I turn again to her and bow low. "Forgive my manners. It's just that I've never seen someone as lovely as you before."

Her soft, pink lips part beneath my gaze and curve up into a stunning smile. She blushes and lowers her eyes. "Thank you."

I grin, glad to have given her a compliment that made her happy. It is true. She is the most beautiful female I've ever beheld. And I am glad I told her, even if nothing can ever come of it. In truth, she has already ruined me for all others. I will never want anyone else now that I have met her. I shall die celibate. For who could ever appeal to me now?

I will be her faithful guard for the remainder of my days. And when I die, it will be with her name upon my lips.

Kai arches a brow at me, and I give him an icy glare. "What?"

"Ella just asked you another question." His voice fails to hide his mirth.

I'm known for getting lost in my head from time to time, and it seems being so enraptured with her has caused me to do it again. "Forgive me." I stare deep into her lovely blue eyes. "What did you ask of me?"

"I asked how to spell your name."

My brows go up in surprise, but I spell it for her anyway. "Why did you wish to know this?"

She looks at me as if my question is absurd. "Because if you are one of my guards, I should know how to spell your name, shouldn't I? It's important to me to get it right."

My heart stops again. Ella is as thoughtful and caring as she is lovely; I am a lost male indeed.

As my gaze travels over the room, it seems that I am not the only one who is lost here either. Each of my brothers gaze at her longingly. After she has been married off to the prince, I suspect each of us will die old and alone. For who could ever find a mate to compare with this perfect creature before us?

My thoughts return to my nightmares of the Wolf Queen murdering her. As I look to Ella, I know for a fact that each and every one of us would die before we'd allow any harm to come to her. I care not if the Wolf Queen made herself the ruler of our kingdom. If she dares try to harm Ella, we will make certain she pays with her life.

CHAPTER 8

DEVON

I t is easy to see that Ella still has many questions for us, but she is exhausted. She makes us promise not to leave while she sleeps. As if we would ever even do such a thing. But then my heart clenches when she thanks us with tears in her eyes simply for being here.

She has only just met us, and already, she treats us as if we are treasured. In truth, we are the ones who should be treating her this way. Fate was generous indeed when it chose us to guard her.

Already, I can sense the tightening of the bonds between us now that we have found her. If it is already this powerful, I cannot imagine how much stronger it will be once she seals us to her. I can think of nothing I would rather do with my life than ensure she is always safe.

Well... actually, I can think of one other thing. I would love to take Ella as my mate. But that goes entirely against our mission. Besides, why would she want any of us when she will marry the prince?

More specifically, why would she ever want *me*? I am a cat shifter. Our kind is usually not wanted. Many females fear us because of how we mark our mates. The ones who are brave enough to be with us suffer the mark's pain during the first mating.

But it does not matter because Ella will be queen once she marries the prince. She is not destined to be with any of us. It will have to be enough to know that a wonderful life will be hers after we help her catch his eye at the ball.

I have never laid eyes upon the male, but already I both hate and envy him. He is the most blessed of all males to be destined for her. Of this, I am certain.

As she lies nestled between Cash and Finn, Kai and Nyx each sleep at the top and the foot of the bed, respectively, leaving nowhere for me, of course.

I am always the odd one out. I do not think they do this on purpose; it is merely the way of things.

So, I lie down just inside the door to guard against any unwanted visitors. Ella assured us that her family never comes up here, but I will be waiting if they do. And I promise to make them pay for every mark and lash upon her back. I can hardly wait for morning to come. With it will come the justice my Ella rightfully deserves. My vow.

The first of the sun's rays peeking over the horizon brings the sound of a carriage. It seems Ella's family has only just returned from wherever they were last night. I get to my feet, ready to descend the stairs, when something nudges at my consciousness.

I turn, thinking it is one of my bond brothers but am surprised when I see Ella staring straight at me.

"Where are you going?" her soft voice asks across the bond.

I am her guard, which means I should hold nothing back from she whom I serve and protect. I meet her blue eyes evenly. *"I am going to make your stepfamily pay for all the wrongs they've done to you."*

She shakes her head. "No," she speaks aloud, startling my bond brothers sleeping around her. "Don't hurt them."

"Why not?" I ask, unable to hide the confusion in my voice. *"They* have hurt you many times."

She sits up, wincing as she does. "Because to do so would make us as horrible as them. And that's not what I want. That's not who I am."

I stand taller, lifting my head. "No, you are not. But that is why you have me. Why you have all of us." I allow my gaze to travel over my brothers. "We are here to do what you cannot, to protect you."

Kai gives me a confused look and opens his mouth to speak but stops when she stands. "I said 'no,'" she hisses. "I will not allow you to do to them what they've done to me. I wouldn't wish this even on my worst enemy."

My hands curl into fists at my side as I think about the marks across her back. They are many, and they are deep. The several scars that crisscross her delicate flesh tell me her stepmother has beaten her many times before. Murderous thoughts fill my mind as I think about the one who did this to her. I want to end her stepmother for daring to even touch her.

But I cannot disobey the order of the one I vowed to serve and protect. "Fine," I grit through my teeth. "They will remain untouched as you have asked."

Anger burns through me. Ella's heart is too tender for this world. It is a weakness to allow an enemy to live. I spin toward the door to start for the stairs.

Kai's voice calls out to me through the bond. *"Where are you going?"*

"To procure a dress," I snap, turning back to face him.

His blue eyes widen at my sharp tone. He may be a blue jay and I am a cat, but he is a fierce warrior and commands respect from all who know him.

Thinking better of showing my irritation to our leader, I dip my chin in a subtle bow. *"I will not disobey her word, if that is what you are worried about."*

He is silent for so long it worries me that I may have gone too far. But after a moment, he replies. *"Be careful, brother."*

I concentrate on shifting my form so that I appear to be wearing clothing. A fine suit of blue with white trim to give me the appearance of a wealthy gentleman. With my eyes downcast, no one should notice anything strange.

This is the only thing that troubles me about being a cat shifter in the human world. No matter my form, my eyes stay the same. Green eyes with vertically slit pupils that betray what I am to any who see them. However, it matters not, for I know exactly where I am going, and the person I plan to meet with will understand what I am and not question me.

The market is bustling with activity. I have never seen it so busy before. Not that I come to the human world very often. But when I have in the past, it has never been this much of a hive of activity.

Everywhere I turn, it is difficult not to bump into people. As I make my way through the crowds, I soon realize why. Everyone is talking about the royal ball. As a result, the dressmaker's shop is much busier than I expected. Several women are lined up outside the door, waiting their turn to get in.

I know it would only be proper to wait my turn, but I am impatient, and Ella is the Chosen One. *She* is the reason for this ball in the first place. The rest of these women do not realize they are wasting their time entertaining thoughts of catching the prince's eye. Once he sees Ella, all others will pale before her beauty, and he will be just as lost as I am.

I sigh as I consider this. It is our mission to ensure they end up together, but deep down, it feels wrong. What if he is not the male that she wants? What if we push them together and she ends up miserable?

After all, the prince is royalty, and from what I've observed of the Wolf Queen and her pack, they are not always the most considerate of people because they are so used to having their way.

The moment I walk into the store, the owner lifts her head and stares directly at me. "Sir!" she calls out. "I have your order ready in the back. If you would, please follow me."

I drop my chin in acknowledgment and follow her through a small door to the back of her building.

As soon as we're alone, she spins to face me with a thunderous expression. "Why are you here?" she practically hisses. "You know it is dangerous."

Unfazed by her anger, I arch a condescending brow. "Is it not dangerous for you to own and run a shop in the human world, being what you are?" I gesture to her form.

Although she appears human to everyone else, a shifter could recognize Rina for what she is a mile away. The vibrant blues and golds of her dress are a clever concealment for her lovely tailfeathers. Their beautiful plumage is quite a sight when they are on full display. I should know. She tried to tempt me once, this peacock shifter.

It was during her heat cycle. Impossible as it may seem, she had her eye on me as her mate in her desperation to sate her need. But I put that notion to rest by gently refusing her with the explanation that I'd been assigned to guard the Chosen One. My life will never fully be my own.

In truth, I did not feel any pull toward her, and I'm confident we would have made a poor match. Especially once her heat cycle ended and she fully returned to herself. She said as much when she thanked me later for not taking advantage of her in that state.

A young boy walks in and takes her hand. He smiles up at me, and I note the soft downy feathers concealed beneath his façade. It seems she found a mate after all, and I am glad for her.

At least she gets her happy ending, whereas I am to forever follow Ella, knowing she can never be mine.

I drop to one knee before the child. "How do you do, young man?"

His mouth curves up in a grin. "Are you like us?" he asks excitedly. His eyes fill with a wonder that I am not used to getting as a cat. Usually, my kind are viewed with slight fear or disgust. It must not be very often that he gets to interact with others of our kind outside of his family.

"Yes."

His smile grows even brighter. "Do you live here too?"

"No, I'm just visiting."

He sticks out his hand for me to shake it. When I do, he grins. "Nice to meet you."

I smile back at him and ruffle his hair. "You too, young man."

He grins again and then skips away back to the front of the store.

I know why Rina and her husband live here. This is the only place they can make a fair living for their child. After all, what use do shifters have for clothing when we can manifest it on ourselves if we desire?

This is why most shifters who risk living in the human

world do so. Because the trade passed down for generations by their family left them no choice. Rina's great grandfather used to clothe the human royal family back during that time. I wonder if she still provides their clothing for them as well.

"What do you need?" she asks.

"A dress. Something to catch the eye of the prince."

Her eyes widen. "Is it for *her*?" she asks, and I understand she means Ella—the Chosen One.

I nod, not wanting to speak her name aloud. Who knows what eyes and ears are spying on us, searching for information about our Chosen One. She was already attacked by one wolf shifter; the deceased shifter's pack will be searching for him soon enough, if not already.

"Of course." She claps her hands together excitedly. "I would be honored to create one for her." Her gaze scans the room, searching the various bolts of fabric as if trying to decide which to choose. She looks back up at me. "Describe her, and I shall make a dress to highlight her attributes."

I lift a thoughtful gaze to the ceiling as I picture Ella. "Long golden hair that is fine like silk. Smooth, pale skin. A slight and delicate frame. Luminous, ocean-blue eyes. Lovely and delicate brows, nose, and cheekbones that give her a fragile appearance, but it belies the strength of steel underneath," I add, thinking of the marks across her back. "Charming and elegant, she—" I stop abruptly, realizing I've gone into far too much detail.

When I look back down at Rina, her lips tip up in a smirk. "It seems you have lost yourself, haven't you, Devon?" She asks with a teasing glint in her eye. "Your head has been turned by a human."

I purse my lips. It is forbidden for a shifter to take a human mate. This rule was in place long before the great war and the divide that followed between our two peoples.

There has been so much bloodshed between us

throughout our history. Humans used to hunt and kill our kind, and any they deemed different, including witches—humans possessing the gift of magic.

It was believed that only shifters possessed magical abilities, and so any humans found to have this power were thought to be in league with us and murdered by their own kind for witchcraft.

What the humans did not realize is that my kind killed witches as well because they were seen as an abomination. Many shifters believe humans should not possess any magical powers.

That is yet another reason why I fear so much for Ella. The prophecy states that the Chosen One has powers of some sort—the ability to heal the land. The Elders do not understand exactly what form of power this is, however. They only know what the ancient texts have said. And Ella's ability to communicate with us through mind speech could be deemed witchcraft by the humans as well.

I clench my jaw as frustration burns through me. She will have enemies on both sides. I only pray that we are strong enough to protect her and that the prince accepts her without question. Surely such a powerful person, with the whole of his kingdom behind him, could help keep her safe as well.

Rina flips her hair behind her shoulder and flashes a mischievous grin at me, pulling me back from my troubled thoughts. "At least it is not just any human you are smitten with. It is the Chosen One, so I suppose there's that."

I narrow my eyes. "You know it is forbidden to mate a human. Besides... as the Chosen One, she is to marry the prince."

"Oh, stop. You know I am only teasing you." Her expression turns serious. "How do you plan to pay for this dress?"

Closing my eyes, I concentrate, allowing the magic to

flow through me. I think about which of my possessions I wish to retrieve before opening my hand. I feel it materialize a moment later. A perfect, green gemstone about half the size of my palm. All shifters carry their items this way. It is necessary to learn this magic at a young age so that we are always free to shift without worrying about any items we may wish to carry.

Rina's mouth drops as her eyes widen in shock. "You are too generous." She tips her head in thanks. "I will make the finest dress to turn the head of the prince."

"Thank you," I reply, hoping that she makes Ella the most beautiful dress in all the kingdom. That gemstone was my most valuable possession. I hate that I must use it to dress Ella to attract the eye of another male. Would that I could have given this gem to her instead as a courting gift. To ask her to be mine.

"It will be ready tomorrow," Rina says, pulling me back from my errant thoughts.

I turn and wave as I leave the building. With a heavy sigh, I head back to the estate. Rina is right. Although I only just met her, I am lost indeed when it comes to Ella.

CHAPTER 9

ELLA

Devon leaves, and I hate that he's angry. It bothers me to know he is upset with my decision, but I will not change my mind. I refuse to be cruel to anyone, even if they've been awful to me. That's not who I am, nor is it who I wish to be.

It's strange how he is human, appearing like the rest. He's tall, with broad shoulders, short-cropped black hair, and a masculine square jaw that could cut glass. And just like his bond brothers, his entire body is chiseled muscular perfection. But his eyes are different. Even in his human form, they remain green vertically slit pupils. I think again of how he stared at me in disbelief when I asked him not to hurt my stepmother.

I look to Kai. "Where did he go?"

His sparkling blue eyes meet mine. "To find you a dress." He tips his head to the side as he studies me. "You did need one, did you not?"

"Oh." And now I feel even worse about our parting. He was leaving to do something nice for me. I hate that I practically snapped at him over him wanting to punish my stepmother. "Yes, I did."

"Do not worry, Ella," Kai adds. "Devon is... Devon."

My brow furrows as my gaze rakes over Kai's form. He gives me a bright smile as he leans on the door. His short, golden hair reflects brightly in the light. His tall, lean, muscular form is gorgeous—like something carved from stone and too perfect to be real.

Finn's warm hands on my shoulders draw my attention back to him. "You need not worry, Ella." He smiles. "Devon is a cat. It is in his nature to be moody."

Cash lightly touches my back. I look over my shoulder and raise my eyebrow in a silent question.

"We should change this dressing."

I sigh and lift my arms, allowing them to unwrap my torso to expose my back. The cool air raises small goosebumps across my exposed flesh, turning my nipples into hardened beads. My cheeks flush warm in embarrassment. But I don't try to hide from their eyes because I know they'd never touch me without my permission. The same bond that makes me feel connected to them also tells me that I can trust them with my life.

I cannot help but notice the way Nyx stares at me, his warm, honey-brown eyes studying me intently. As soon as he notices my gaze upon him, his face flares bright red, and he lowers his gaze. His chestnut brown hair falls forward, the length just barely above his brow.

As I observe him, I still cannot believe these big, muscular men can turn into creatures so small. Despite that he can shift into a rabbit, Nyx's human form is thick layers of muscle, not an ounce of fat on his body, from what I can see.

He clenches his jaw as he stares at me with a pained expression. "Does it hurt, Ella?" he asks softly.

"It feels much better now," I reply. It's the truth. The medicine they placed on my injuries has helped me tremendously.

Cash pulls me against him, smoothing his hands up and down my arms, while Finn cleans and applies more of the poultice to my wounds. It feels so good to be taken care of for once. I can't remember the last time someone did anything like this for me.

A sharp voice calls up from down below. "Ella!"

I still.

Cash hugs me even tighter.

"Ella, get down here! We need you!" my stepmother calls out. "I didn't beat you *that* badly yesterday, for goodness sake!"

Cash growls low in his chest. So does everyone else. The room is full of deep, rumbling noises of anger.

Kai puts a hand on my shoulder. "Do you want us to—"

I don't let him finish the sentence. He doesn't understand. None of them do. It's easier just to do whatever she asks of me. After all, I have nowhere else to go if she kicks me out. Or do I?

I look back at him with a renewed hope. "You said you're my guards. Can you... take me away from here?"

He lowers his gaze and shakes his head softly. "Until our two kingdoms are at peace, we cannot take you back to our world. It is forbidden to part the veil for a human."

"Oh." I force myself to bite back my disappointment.

Steeling myself, I stand. Pain shoots through me, but I grit my teeth and remain silent. It does no good to complain. I allow my gaze to drift over each of them. "I'll be downstairs doing my chores. But as soon as I finish, I'll come back up here. Don't worry. She never comes up here, so you should all be well hidden."

I move to my dresser and pull out a fresh work dress and apron. I move behind my room divider and change into my clothes. When I emerge, I watch as each of them shifts into their animal forms. It's so strange to see them so small like this when they are anything but in their human forms.

"We'll help you," Finn looks up at me in his chipmunk form as he speaks in my mind, and I smile.

I'm still not used to hearing them in my thoughts, but it's comforting, in a way, to have such an intimate connection to them. *"All right. But be careful that you remain out of sight."*

They follow behind me as I go down the stairs, and when I start breakfast, everyone pitches in where they can. They shift back into human form to help me clean, mindful of staying hidden where no one but me can see them.

As I'm cleaning up the breakfast table, my stepmother turns to me. "We'll need you to take us into town tomorrow."

My heart stops. "Me?" I smile. She never asks me to go with them anywhere, and I'm excited to be included for once.

"Yes." She smirks. "We'll need someone to carry the packages for us."

My expression falls. "Oh. Of course."

After I finish clearing the table, I move back into the kitchen to tell my guards that I'll be gone tomorrow, but it seems they've already heard. Kai's blue eyes meet mine. "We will go with you."

"How?"

"It's easy to remain hidden when we shift." He chuckles as he uses his hands and gestures how small he would be. "You'll see."

I grin. "All right. I trust you."

I move to the back door to lock it but stop when I notice

a black cat approach. "Devon?" He shifts almost instantly then walks the last two steps to greet me in the doorway.

"Were you mad at me earlier?" I ask because I have to know. I don't like to part with anyone in anger. Father taught me it was not good to hold on to negative emotions.

Devon blinks down at me a moment before answering. He's so tall. Then again, all of them are. Only there's something about him that's different from the rest. Yes, his eyes are cat-like, but it's more than that. It's his presence. He moves with a sort of lethal grace that belies his heavily muscled form. He stares down at me with an intensity that makes my heart stop then quicken its pace.

"I want to apologize for earlier," he says, his voice deep and smooth.

"Oh, that's all right," I reply, stepping back to allow him to pass. "You were only acting out of concern and—"

"I meant how I walked away from you and just left," he interrupts, halting my retreat. "It was wrong of me. I was angry, but not at you." His green eyes meet mine as he reaches out and touches my cheek. The tips of his fingers leaving a heated trail in their wake. "I could never be mad at you, Ella. Forgive me."

"I do. I just—" I lower my gaze, unsure what to say before finally settling on, "want us never to leave one another in anger." I lift my eyes back to him. "Agreed?"

A ghost of a smile tugs at his lips. "Agreed."

I walk outside, and he follows me to the gardens as I tend to the vegetable beds.

My stepfamily retires to their sitting room as they usually do with the tea I've laid out for them, so I know we won't be interrupted. Even so, I turn back when I notice the rest of my guards following us as well.

"You should all probably shift while we're out here," I warn them. "Just in case."

In the blink of an eye, they all transform.

I smile because, all together like this, they look as if they're posing for some sort of whimsical painting. A rabbit, a blue jay, a cat, and two chipmunks. All of us surrounded by carefully manicured gardens full of vibrant flowering plants in an assortment of blues, reds, whites, and yellows.

The bushes are all trimmed neatly in rows, and the vegetable garden is thriving with thick vines full of ripe, red tomatoes ready to be picked.

As I work on harvesting some of the vegetables, I smile up at Devon. He's lounging on the edge of the fountain in a very cat-like pose of feigned indifference to the world around him. Nyx comes up behind him with a mischievous look in his eyes and a slight twitch of his rabbit nose as he studies the cat. He carefully hops toward Devon, and I wonder what he's up to. Without warning, he kicks out at the cat shifter, knocking him into the water. A loud hiss rings in the air.

A startled laugh escapes me, but I quickly cover my mouth to silence it as Devon pulls himself out of the fountain, dripping wet and looking for all the world to see that he is a miserable cat, indeed.

Devon reaches up to swipe at Nyx, but the rabbit rushes to my side and settles against me. I arch a teasing brow. "You expect *me* to keep you safe?" I ask. "I thought *you* were supposed to be my guard, not the other way around."

"*I simply wished to be at your side,*" he teases in my head.

Devon flicks his long, black tail in agitation. "*Just try that again and see what happens, rabbit.*"

Nyx turns away, ignoring him as he nestles against me. He's so fluffy, I want to pet him, but I'm not sure that's entirely appropriate since he's technically a man. So, I don't.

Kai swoops down and lands in front of me. His blue eyes

search mine a moment before he moves closer, settling down against me on the opposite side of Nyx. Finn and Cash come over and do the same.

I smile at them and then glance back up at Devon, wondering if he'll come over here too.

Instead, he stretches out on the low stone wall as if trying to dry himself in the sun. He closes his eyes.

"Are you going to take a nap?" I ask.

"I'm a light sleeper," he replies. *"I will know if anyone approaches."* He flicks one ear in our direction. *"That includes you, rabbit."*

I laugh. His reply was such a cat thing to say.

Sighing, I look out at the garden and the fields beyond the low wall. Everything is so dry here lately. It's depressing. It used to be green fields as far as the eye can see, but almost everything is dull and beginning to turn brown these past few years. Everywhere but the estate and much of the forest that borders it, it seems.

I look back down at my vegetables then start to sing, trying to lighten my mood. It does no good to dwell on negative things, after all.

As I sing, Kai joins in. His voice smooth and velvety in my head as the words flow through my mind while I hear his bird song aloud as well.

The sky grows dark, and clouds begin roiling overhead as the wind picks up. Lightning arcs across the sky. Booming thunder rumbles above us a moment before the sky opens up, and thick droplets of rain begin pelting the ground.

I quickly gather my basket full of vegetables. All the guys shift forms, and together we race toward my tower. The heavy rain drenches me by the time we step inside. My guards follow close behind me as we ascend the stairs back to my room.

When we reach the top, I realize that my dress is completely soaked through. The fabric is so threadbare it leaves nothing to the imagination. Normally, I would not care, but I notice several pairs of eyes staring at me with strange expressions I cannot quite discern.

Someone places a towel over my shoulders, and I look back to find Finn standing behind me. His light brown hair slightly disheveled and wet from the rain, hangs down over his brow. His warm green eyes meet mine in concern. "You should change out of these wet things, Ella, so we can redress your wounds."

I move back behind the screen. When I start to lift my dress off, the wet fabric clings to my injuries, and a small whimper of pain escapes me.

To my shock, everyone rushes to see what's wrong. Partially undressed, I gape at them, embarrassed.

Finn's words set me at ease, though. "It's all right, Ella. We only want to help you. Please," he says. "Let us take care of you."

Nervous, I tuck a stray tendril of hair behind my ear. "I know. Just... allow me to change into my nightshift first, all right?"

"As you wish."

Without another word, they all leave again.

It's so strange being here with so many people, especially men. Before I met them, I'd never spent as much time in the company of any man save my father when I was still a child.

When I finish changing, I come back out, and they motion for me to lie on my stomach on the bed. Cautiously, they lift my nightshift, careful to cover my backside with the blanket so as not to expose me.

Warm hands travel over my back as they cleanse and tend to my wounds. They're so gentle with me. The poultice is like a soothing balm over my injuries, taking away all my discomfort. I close my eyes as they carefully apply the wrap around my torso.

When finished, they lie down beside me. It's cold in here from the many holes in the walls and the rafters, but as they press in around me, I sigh in contentment at their soothing warmth. I inhale their masculine scents—a strange mixture of chocolate and cinnamon. It's wonderful, and I close my eyes, reveling in the sensation of being cared for and protected.

When have I ever felt so loved and safe?

Strong arms drape across my waist as I lie on my side and tug me closer. I realize it's Finn, and I snuggle into his chest. "Thank you, Finn."

Cash settles behind me, holding me close as well.

Finn's green eyes meet mine with a curious look. "How do you do that?"

"Do what?"

"Tell us apart so easily?"

I reach across and brush the hair back from his brow. "Your eyes," I tell him. "Yours are a bit more serious. While Cash's," I turn to him and touch his face, "look more mischievous."

Nyx lies down by my feet and Kai near my head. His blue gaze holds mine as he gently runs his fingers through my hair and sings softly to me. He really does have a lovely, deep voice. Smooth and rich like velvet.

I open my eyes to find Devon staring down at us. Something flickers across his face, but it's gone so quickly I'm uncertain what it is. I do feel bad for him, however. He didn't sleep with us last night, and I don't want him to feel left out.

I lift my arm to him, and he takes my hand. "Lie down with us."

His ordinarily stern expression softens, and he lies on the other side of Finn. I reach my hand out to take his, and he entwines our fingers as I close my eyes and allow myself to drift away, surrounded by my guards.

Awareness slowly trickles back into my mind. I nestle deeper into Finn's embrace, and Cash tightens his arm around me from behind. It feels so good to be held. I lift my head, and Finn's green eyes meet mine. He gives me a sleepy smile then tenderly kisses my forehead. "Did you sleep well?"

"Yes." I reach up and trace my finger across the beautiful line of his jaw. "I like this," I whisper. "Being here with all of you. I feel... close to you all even though we just met. I know you say it's the bond, but it... it feels like something more."

Kai runs his fingers gently through my hair in a soothing gesture. "With time, the bond will only strengthen."

I take his hand, threading my fingers through his as I meet his blue eyes. "Will it always be this way between us?" I ask. "This closeness like we have now?"

His gaze flicks to Finn's for a moment before he answers. Sadness flits briefly across his expression. "The bond will remain, and we will always be your guards. But this"—he gestures to each of the others—"we... cannot always remain with you like this."

His answer troubles me. "Why not?"

Finn touches my cheek, his green eyes staring at me like I'm a rare and precious treasure. "We will remain at your side and we will always protect you, Ella. But you are to marry the prince. He is human. He will not tolerate this level of... closeness."

I lower my gaze. I suppose he's right. What husband would ever allow his wife to sleep surrounded by men? Even if they were her bonded guards?

"I don't understand, though," I mutter. "How will my marrying the prince help unite the two kingdoms?"

Kai smiles warmly. "You are the Chosen One. You will broker peace between the two kingdoms through marriage. Your ability to understand us through our mind speech in both human and animal forms is a gift. One that will help bridge the divide between humans and shifters.

"The prophecy foretells that you will teach the prince of us and through you, he will become more accepting... more understanding of who and what we are. He will see that we are not the demonic beasts many of the humans believe us to be."

It's strange to think that someone like me. A person of very little importance would be the key to something so critical.

"Can't we simply just request an audience with him?" I ask. "Speak to him of a truce?"

Kai shakes his head.

"Why?"

He tenderly cups my cheek, brushing the pad of his thumb across my skin. "Because the Elders have foreseen it. Only through marriage to the Chosen One will his eyes be opened to our world and the path to peace."

Finn smooths his hand down my arm. "Do you not want to be a princess, Ella?"

I lower my gaze. "I just... I don't know what kind of man the prince may be."

"He must be good," Kai offers, and yet, in his blue eyes, I can see a hint of doubt. "If not, the Elders would have seen problems in your match to him."

"Thank you, Kai. That makes me feel a bit better."

I lie there a moment more, enjoying their presence and the feel of their comforting warmth all around me. Tonight is the royal ball. If the prince chooses me as they hope, he will take me as his bride right then and there. I will be sealed to him this evening.

I'm nervous, but I trust Kai and the others when they say this is how it's supposed to be. They are my guards. They're bonded to me and take care of me. They would never lead me down the wrong path. Of this, I am sure. I know it deep in my soul.

CHAPTER 10

KAI

Cash and Finn slip into Ella's pocket, in their chipmunk forms, before she enters the carriage with her stepfamily, while Devon and Nyx hide beneath the bench, concealed behind Ella's long dress.

I fly overhead, making sure to keep them in sight at all times as we make our way into the city.

When we reach the dressmaker, Devon and Nyx remain in the carriage. After all, a cat and a rabbit are too conspicuous to remain hidden like the rest of us are. I shift into my human form behind the building, making sure to appear as if I am wearing the elegant coat and pants of a wealthy gentleman. I choose a deep blue color to highlight my golden hair and blue eyes. Several ladies stare at me appreciatively as I enter the shop, but I pay them no mind as I search for Ella.

When I find her, I move to her side and then lean down and whisper in her ear. "Ask for the owner. Her name is Rina. Tell her that Devon sent you to pick up a dress."

She smiles. "Is it my dress for the ball?"

"Yes. He paid handsomely for it. So I'm sure it will be a beautiful design."

I scan the shop, watching for any danger as Ella goes off to find Rina. A woman comes from out of the back a moment later. My eyes widen slightly as soon as I see the peacock shifter.

Devon told me what she was, but it is strange to see a fellow shifter on this side of the veil. No wonder these dresses are so in demand. Only a creature of great beauty could create such gorgeous designs in turn. Rina hands her a package, and Ella places it in one of the many bags she is already carrying for her stepfamily.

It disturbs me how terrible they treat her. Even more troubling is how Ella accepts it as her life. She must have endured many things over the years. I wish we had been sent to her sooner.

Ella loses her grip on one of the bags, and it slips to the floor. Her stepmother slaps her hard across the cheek. "Clumsy girl! Mind what you are doing!"

My hands curl into fists at my side as anger rolls through me. I wish we could take Ella away from all this to our cottage in the woods. But it is forbidden to take a human beyond the veil. If we were discovered, the punishment would be severe.

I shake my head. The price is too high. We cannot risk taking her there.

Besides, I think to myself bitterly, she will catch the eye of the prince this night. And once she does, she will be royalty, and no one will ever harm her again.

Her stepmother raises her hand again, and I step between them, wrapping my hand around her forearm, stopping her abruptly. "Do not touch her," I grind out.

Anger burns through me like fire as I stare down at her.

84

"I—I... she's my stepdaughter, sir. I was only disciplining her."

Holding her gaze, I lean down and whisper in her ear. "Do it again and you shall discover I possess a wrath like none you could possibly imagine."

I relinquish my grip on her forearm, and she pulls away, her entire face completely pale. "Of—of course," she says, and turns quickly to head back to the carriage.

Ella casts a glance at me over her shoulder, and I give her a bright smile. I know she did not want us to do anything unkind to her stepmother, but I also know she could not possibly have heard what I whispered in her stepmother's ear.

And to be honest, even if she had, I would not take it back. I cannot stand to watch that woman abuse Ella. None of us can, and it ends now. I know Ella does not want us to interfere, but we are her guards, and we will protect her even if it means protecting her from her so-called family.

When we finally return to the estate, I fly up to the window ledge and watch as Ella struggles to unload all the parcels and packages. She carries them up the stairs of the estate and to her stepfamily's rooms.

Her stepsisters make her dress them and fix their hair. All the while they make comments about her tattered clothing, bragging to her that they will enthrall the prince this evening with their feminine charms.

I'm not sure what they are speaking of because there is absolutely nothing charming, feminine, or beautiful about either of them. There is a reason why they are still eligible.

She helps her stepmother ready herself as well, and by the

time she returns to the tower, it is easy to see she is exhausted.

Having observed how she readied her stepfamily, each of us decide to do the same for her.

"Please." I bow low. "Allow us to help you get ready for the ball."

She smiles. "Thank you. That would be lovely."

When she opens the package with her dress, her eyes widen, and she beams across at Devon. In this moment, I am utterly jealous that she directs her gorgeous smile at him. How will I bear it when she looks at her husband, the prince, in this way?

"It's perfect, Devon!" she exclaims, and then wraps her arms around him in a hug. "I absolutely love it. The prince is sure to notice me in this."

His expression falls slightly, but he quickly recovers and bows low. "I am pleased you like it."

Cash and Finn draw her a bath, filling the old washtub she has in the corner. I hate that this is the best we can offer her. With no way to heat the water, I'm certain it must be cold, but she does not complain. Instead, she thanks us from behind her room divider.

I was glad to note, however, that the poultice worked. The marks on her back are now completely closed.

When she emerges wrapped only in a towel, her long silken hair is wet and clings to her body. Tiny rivulets of water run down her neck to the valley between her breasts, disappearing beneath the fabric of the towel, which seems to hug and accentuate every curve of her form.

She takes the slip gown from my hands and goes behind her divider to dry off and change into it.

When she emerges, it takes all my effort not to gape at her. The slip, although it covers her body, only comes down to mid-thigh. It is made of fine white silk to go beneath her dress, but the fabric is so light it is almost completely sheer.

My hands ache with want to touch her. I have never been with a female. None of my brothers have either. It is easy to see in their gazes the same desire and longing I'm sure I express in mine. I force myself to look away as I gather her dress.

She is not mine.

She is ours to protect and defend, but that is all. We can never be more than this to her.

I do not know him, but I already dislike the prince. He had better treat her like the great treasure that she is and never take her for granted as royalty is oft to do when given something so precious. If he does not, he will answer to us.

The sound of a carriage below draws my attention as a shrill voice cries up toward the tower. "Don't bother waiting up for us, Ella!" one of her sisters mocks. "I'll probably call for you in the morning after I've married the prince!"

Ella's eyes lock onto mine. "How will I get to the ball without a carriage?"

Nyx bows low. "Leave it to us. We will get you there. Do not worry."

I love that she trusts us enough not to ask anything further. She accepts what we tell her to be true. It is good that she has this deep connection to us. I've heard that it can take guards and their female many moons to form a bond as strong as this. The fact that we have one already means fate was wise in choosing us to be hers.

CHAPTER 11

KAI

I stare at Ella as Nyx fixes her hair. He pulls it up into an intricate design of twists and braids atop her head, leaving half of it down to cascade over her back and shoulders. The dress, made of fine silk, is light blue and seems to sparkle and shimmer like pale starlight.

Her shoulders and neckline are bare and exposed as the fabric dips to the "V" of her breasts, accentuating the soft, creamy mounds that peak over the material. My fingers ache with the want to touch her delicate skin. But I must quell this hunger and desire that burns brightly in me because she will never be my mate.

The *clip-clop* of hooves downstairs draws her attention, and she turns back to us with a questioning gaze.

Devon steps forward. "I have procured a ride for you to the castle, along with two chaperones."

She gives him a puzzled look and starts for the stairs, but he stops her abruptly. "I have something else for you as well," he adds.

"What is it?"

Closing his eyes, Devon calls upon magic to materialize his possessions. A pearl necklace appears in his hands. He smiles and offers it to her.

"This is for me?" She stares at the necklace in wonder. "It's too much. I—I cannot accept this, Devon."

"Please." He bows low. "I want you to have it."

She hesitates a moment, and then turns her back to him. Carefully, she lifts her hair from her shoulders. "Do you mind putting it on me?"

Does he mind? That sly cat. I should've known he would take this opportunity to show off with such lavish gifts. He probably anticipated this exact request, knowing he'd be allowed to touch her. Red fills my vision as his hands linger a bit longer than necessary at the nape of her neck.

To my surprise, Cash and Finn offer her a pair of earrings to go with it. Those devious chipmunks must have collaborated with him on these gifts.

They confirm my suspicions a moment later when they smile and then dip their chins at him, and he does the same in return as she clips the earrings on.

Never one to be outdone, I glance down at her shoes. These will not do for such a fine gown. I summon my possessions for the items I've been saving for my mate. I know now that I will never have one, because no one else will ever compare to Ella.

I hold out a pair of glass slippers to her. She stares at them in wonder. "Are these made of glass?"

"Not just any glass," I tell her. "Enchanted crystal. It will mold to your foot and allow you to move with ease as you walk."

I kneel beside her, and she carefully lifts her skirt just enough to extend her delicate feet out to me. Shamelessly, I cup her calves with one hand while I fit the shoes with the other.

Her skin is soft, supple, and smooth beneath her silken stockings, and I long to skim the tips of my fingers up her legs to her thighs and—

"They're lovely," she exclaims, pulling me back from my errant thoughts. "Thank you, Kai."

Cash and Finn narrow their eyes behind her, for they know I have outdone their gift by far.

While I am happy to give her gifts, I can hardly bear to think that the things we offer her are to help her catch *his* eye. It feels wrong to lead her to the prince in this way, especially when everything inside me screams that she should be mine.

I look to my bond brothers. No. She should be *ours*.

I force myself to focus. It is Ella's destiny to marry the prince. Not us. "We must leave," I tell her and usher her to the door.

When we reach the carriage downstairs, I smile in greeting to the peacock shifter, Rina, and her mate, Malen. "Thank you for helping us," I tell them.

They bow low. "It is our honor to help the Chosen One."

I help Ella into the carriage, and we all climb in beside her. We are fortunate it is large enough to accommodate us in our human forms so that we may ride with her in this way.

As we bump along the road into town, I study each of my bond brothers. Concentrating on the connection between us, I want to make sure Ella cannot hear me before I reach out to their minds.

I gaze at Cash and Finn, the twins looking more somber than I've ever seen them before. "*Tonight, if all goes well, everything changes. You all understand this, right?*"

"*Yes,*" they each respond, although I note Cash and Finn are a bit hesitant in their reply.

"I know it has only been a few days, but it seems we are not immune to the pull of the bond. We are not the first guards to feel possessive toward our female as if she were our mate." I pause. *"But the prince is human. They do not tolerate other males being so familiar with their wives. We are her guards, and that is all that we are. Do you understand?"*

"*Yes*," they each reluctantly agree.

CHAPTER 12

ELLA

I look out the carriage window, marveling at the grandeur of the castle before me. Tall towers capped with silver peaked rooftops reach up toward the sky. The whitewashed stone seems to gleam beneath the last of the golden rays of the sun. If everything goes right this evening, soon this will be my home.

But as I glance at each of my guards, I can't help but feel a sharp pang of sadness in my chest. I don't know if it's the bond that makes me feel this way, but I would not choose the prince if I had the choice. I do not want to give up the close relationship I have already formed with my guards.

They claim it's my destiny to marry the prince and unite our two kingdoms. Perhaps I would have been excited by the prospect before I met my guards. But now that I have them, I can't deny the deep longing I feel in my heart when I think that I'll soon be married off to the prince. That I'll never sleep surrounded by my guards. Never touch them. Never...

I shake my head to clear my thoughts. They probably wouldn't want me anyway. I'm human, and they're shifters.

With a heavy sigh, I turn my attention back to the window. We are almost inside the palace gates. I've never been this close to the castle before. It's much larger than I thought, and as we circle into the courtyard, I notice all the royal guards dressed in their fine black and silver uniforms standing sentry just outside the massive glass and silver doors.

Golden light spills out from inside, casting a soft, ethereal glow to the gardens that surround the entire space. Fine carriages with gold and silver trim line the drive, and I watch in wonder as ladies dressed in elegant gowns line up outside the doors, waiting to be called upon to enter.

I look to my guards. I wish they were coming with me, but Kai says they will guard me from hidden positions throughout the ballroom. He doubts any of the wolf shifters will come for me here, but he wants to remain vigilant just to be certain.

My gaze drifts to Cash and Finn. Although I understand the bond makes me feel close to each of the bonded brothers, I feel much closer to the two chipmunk shifter twins. After all, they were the ones who found me. The ones who have lain by my side for the past few nights. Before I met them, I probably would have been thrilled to be here now and excited to think that I might marry the prince. But now, I find myself wishing I could just live a quiet life somewhere in the woods with my guards, away from everything else.

Finn leans forward and takes my hand, squeezing it gently. His green eyes stare deep into mine as he gives me a faint smile. "The prince is sure to notice you right away. You are beautiful, Ella. He will surely seek you out immediately. And once he does, after speaking with you, he will know what a beautiful mind you have, and he will become completely enraptured with you."

Tears sting my eyes, but I blink them back. "Thank you, Finn." I allow my gaze to travel over the rest of them. "All of you will be inside somewhere with me, right?"

They nod, and I do my best to give them a smile despite my nerves. "Give me some sort of sign so that I might see you, all right?"

"We will," Nyx says.

Devon's eyes are downcast, and his expression is stern. I reach across and place my hand atop his. He lifts his gaze to me, and something akin to sadness flickers behind his green cat eyes. "The dress is lovely, Devon. More beautiful than anything I've ever worn before. Thank you."

A faint smile tilts his lips. "It is you who makes it so, not the material."

I squeeze his hand. "Thank you."

With that, I turn to Rina and her husband. He helps me out of the carriage. As I step onto the courtyard pavers, I notice my guards' small shadows as they exit the carriage in their animal forms.

We line up at the door with everyone else. It feels like forever until we're inside, and as my gaze travels over the grand ballroom, I stare at everything in wonder.

The high dome ceiling covered in silver and gold finishes reflects brilliantly in the light. Several crystal chandeliers hang overhead, the largest one with twelve rows of glittering lights that sparkle like gems.

Couples dance across the floor, the voluminous skirts of the elegant women swaying around them as they keep time with the music, whirling and spinning in a lovely display. But it's the man across the way that catches my attention.

Standing at the top of a winding staircase, he gazes down at the dancers below. Dressed in a deep blue coat and pants, lined with a silver and gold hem, he appears somewhat detached from everything happening around him. The light reflects off his short-cropped hair, making it shine like fine spun gold. As soon as we're announced, he lifts his head.

My name is changed, of course, so as not to alert my step-sisters I am here. I am introduced as Lady Rella, adding an R to my name to keep as close to the original spelling as possible.

His gaze seems to zero in on me as we move on and continue toward the long table full of sparkling goblets of champagne. The strange man starts down the stairs, his eyes locked on me.

"Rella?" Rina's soft voice draws my attention. "Would you like a glass?"

I nod and accept it from her. I take a small sip of the bubbly drink. The sweet and citrus flavor rolls across my tongue, and I've never tasted anything so wonderfully delightful before.

I finish one glass and then drink another. My entire body flushes with warmth and suddenly, I'm no longer quite as nervous as I was before.

A hand on my shoulder draws my attention, and I turn to look up into deep blue eyes. They stare down at me with an almost predatory gaze as they rake over my form. He bows low, his expression stern and unreadable. "Good evening, my lady," he says in a low, smooth voice. "I was wondering if you'd do me the honor of accompanying me during the next song."

The entire room grows silent. Only the sound of stringed instruments from the orchestra fills the air. As his gaze holds mine, everything else falls away as he extends his arm out to me, offering his hand.

Cautiously, I reach for it, and he pulls me toward him. He stares down at me intensely, and my heart slams in my chest as he licks his full perfect lips then drags me even closer until I'm completely flush against his front.

I only have a moment to wonder who he is before hushed whispers sound around us. "The prince," someone says. "He's going to dance with that girl. Who is she?"

Several more voices speak in whispered tones asking similar questions.

"Are you the prince?" I ask because I want to be sure.

His mouth curves up into a devastatingly handsome smile. "Yes, I am. And you are Lady Rella, is that correct?"

I nod. "I... I go by Ella, your grace."

"Ella, then," he says.

His arms band tightly around my waist while his other hand grips mine firmly, entwining our fingers. Deep blue eyes stare down at me, and I blink up at him, unsure what to do.

As if sensing my nervousness, he grins. "Trust me and just follow my lead, Ella."

"All—all right," I stumble over my words.

Something about him makes me uncomfortable. With my guards, I knew instantly that I could trust them. But when the prince asked me the same, my first inclination was to pull away. Instead, I'm allowing him to lead me onto the ballroom floor.

If my guards had not told me of the prophecy, I would probably make an excuse to leave. There is something about the prince that unnerves me. But then again, perhaps it is merely anxiety from being this close to the man destined to become my husband.

He pulls me onto the floor, and we begin to dance and spin. He pushes me slightly to whirl me away before twirling my body back to him. I'm surprised when he pulls me back into his arms and dips me low. One hand behind my back while the other moves up between the valley of my breasts to my neck as he stares down at me like a predator considering its prey.

My chest heaves as I struggle to catch my breath, trying to calm my fluttering heart because I'm so nervous and yet oddly aroused at the same time. No one has ever touched me like this. So intimately. His hand is pressing insistently against my body as he smooths a line down the valley of my breasts. I should slap him for taking such liberties, but perhaps this is what is supposed to happen between and man and the woman he is to marry. I would not know. I've never even been courted.

I scan the room, hoping to see Kai or one of the others for reassurance, but I find nothing. Wherever they are, they are well hidden.

The prince lifts me back up, holding me tightly to his chest as we continue to follow the song's rhythm.

Something hard presses between us, and I gasp when I realize what it is. I may not know much of men, but I do recognize this. His length is like a hard bar against my abdomen. Having noticed my alarm, a smile tugs at his lips. He leans down and whispers in my ear. "I think I'll take you."

I blink up at him, not sure what he means. But he takes my hand firmly in his and leads us off the floor. He grabs two more glasses of that delightful bubbly drink and gives them both to me. They taste so delicious I have no trouble drinking them both.

Several pairs of eyes track us as he pulls me through a narrow door that leads out into the palace gardens. The full moon shines brightly overhead, casting everything in an ethereal silver glow. Thick rows of hedges full of blossoming flowers line the small, cobbled path straight to the center's large fountain. A soft breeze carries the delicate fragrance of the many roses that we pass.

My entire body feels light as a feather, and I gaze in

wonder at the beauty that surrounds us. These gardens are so lovely, I can only imagine how much more beautiful they must be during the day. As we continue moving farther away from the palace, it occurs to me that he and I are entirely alone out here. Despite the lightness of my mood, panic spikes through me. "Your grace," I begin, "what about your guests?"

He guides me back against the massive trunk of a nearby tree, and presses his hips firmly to mine. "They can wait." He grins. "And call me Alexander."

Pinned between him and the tree like this does strange things to me, but I'm nervous. I've never done anything like this before, and I'm not sure what to do. I'm not even certain that I like this odd feeling.

He leans forward and drops his head to the curve of my neck and shoulder. He presses a series of kisses along my sensitive skin. I breathe shakily as his hand moves down my neck to the top of my dress, and he slips his fingers beneath the neckline.

I gasp as he palms my breast, brushing his thumb across the soft peak until it hardens. My entire body lights up beneath his touch, but I... this all seems to be happening too fast.

Kai and the others assured me this man would be my husband, but I'm not sure I want to let him take me before we are wed.

"Alexander, I've never—"

He whispers against my skin. "Then allow me to lead, my lady."

CHAPTER 13

KAI

We follow Ella and the prince out into the royal palace gardens. I sit beside Cash and Finn on a nearby tree, observing. Devon comes up beside us, his black fur nearly invisible against the dark shadows. I project my bitter thoughts to him. *"Your dress seems to have worked. It definitely caught the attention of the prince."*

With a slight clench of his jaw, he says nothing as he continues to stare down at Ella and the prince. The prince drops his head between her neck and shoulder, pressing a line of kisses along her skin.

Nyx makes a soft noise of frustration on the ground near the tree's base then shifts into his human form. I glare down at him as he climbs up beside us. I arch a condescending brow. *"Was that necessary? You risk exposing us all."*

A hint of irritation shifts into his gaze. *"I could not see anything from the ground."*

"What do you need to see?" I ask. *"Can you not tell from our conversation that it is going as planned?"*

He turns to look down at Ella and the prince and he gasps.

The prince dips his hands beneath the neckline of her dress and cups her breast. Nyx growls low in his throat. *"Is it going as planned?"* he asks. *"Does not something seem off to you?"*

"I want you as mine," the prince says in a low voice between presses of his lips to her skin. "Say 'yes,' Ella. Tell me that you will marry me."

"Yes," she says, her voice a breathy sigh as he cups her breast.

My heart shatters at the sight. We should be happy that our plan is working. And yet, I cannot deny that something feels wrong here. But I push the feeling down, believing it to be mere jealousy. I wish it were me pressing tender kisses to her delicate skin. Me cupping her breast in my palm and making her breath rasp as I awaken her desires. Why does it have to be him?

I had not realized I'd projected these thoughts aloud to my bond brothers until Finn comes up beside me and touches my wing. *"I feel the same, brother,"* he says as he turns his gaze to everyone else. *"As do we all."*

"Let us go then and find my parents," the prince murmurs. "I must take you to them since you have agreed to be mine."

Hand in hand, they leave the gardens to head back inside the palace, and we follow silently to bear witness.

CHAPTER 14

ELLA

The prince takes my hand and leads me to the two thrones at the top of the balcony, overlooking the ball. Everyone stops what they are doing and stares, watching us with curious eyes as we approach the king and queen.

The queen stares down at me imperiously, as her gaze moves up and down my form. Her golden hair is twisted up in a series of braids atop her head, and I note the several white strands threading through it. Her eyes are as blue as the ocean, the same as her son's, but there is little warmth in their depths as they move over me.

The king has peppered gray hair and deep brown eyes that seem to look straight through my soul as I stand before them. His features hard and worn with age.

Alexander bows, and I do the same.

"Mother, Father," he begins, "I have chosen Ella to be mine."

The queen arches a condescending brow. "Are you certain

you want *her*? You've not even given the other maidens here a chance."

He squeezes my hand. "I am certain."

I can hardly believe this is real. It's all happening so fast. Did the dressmaker cast some kind of enchantment upon the material? Am I really about to become the princess of the kingdom?

Even as all these thoughts run through my mind, I find myself thinking of my guards.

Of Cash, Finn, Nyx, Kai, and Devon.

The prince is handsome, there's no question about that. But I feel as if I'm betraying my heart by agreeing to be his.

"Very well," the king answers. He stands then moves to the balcony to address the crowd below. "My subjects. I must inform you that my son has made his choice."

His words are greeted with silence and not a few sounds of pitiful sniffling and tears from the many women who realize their chance to become queen someday is now gone.

He continues. "There is still much food and drink to be had. Let us celebrate my son's choice of..." He looks back to us and whispers. "What is your name, my lady?"

"Ella," I reply, deciding to give him my real name because my stepfamily will find out eventually anyway. Might as well let them get used to this now that the prince has chosen me.

"Ella," the king proclaims to the crowd.

The scattered sound of applause rings out below, and the music begins again. I note several people make their way to the doors, realizing their goal for the evening is now unattainable.

The prince tugs on my hand to lead me out into a long hallway. "Where are we going?"

"I'm going to show you to your rooms." He smiles.

"But what about—"

He cuts me off. "Do not worry about your things. We will send for them in the morning. This is your place now."

I note the way he says "place" instead of "home." That's rather odd. I am, however, glad he's taking me to separate rooms. I'm not sure I'm ready just yet to be completely his. I've never made love before, and I'll admit the thought unnerves me. I have heard that the first time can be rather painful, and I... I'm just not sure that I want to rush into something that intimate so quickly. After all, I've only just met the prince—my future husband. Surely, he will understand that I want to know him better before we do something so intimate.

We reach a large door at the end of the hallway, and he pushes it open. I turn, meaning to ask him if he wishes to spend more time talking, but he steps inside with me, locking the door behind him. He moves his hand to my waist and presses me against the wall.

His gaze holds mine as he slides my dress farther down to expose my breasts.

"Alexander, wait, I—"

He cups my breast, running his thumb across the already stiff peak. A soft moan escapes me because it feels so good, igniting a burning deep in my core.

But it's all happening so fast. I want to slow down a bit.

"So responsive," he murmurs. "I like that." He cocks his head to the side. "I assume you are untouched."

Confused, I look down at his hand and he chuckles.

"No other man has ever touched you like this, have they?"

I shake my head, unable to voice my answer.

He grips the skirt of my dress and begins to lift it toward my waist. His fingers skate along my inner thigh and trace lightly over the small scrap of silken fabric between my legs.

I smooth my hands firmly over my skirt to push it and his hand back down.

He gives me a curious look as I smile nervously up at him. "I, uh... thought we might talk for a bit first. I mean... I've never done this before, and I'm a bit nervous and—"

He begins kissing my neck again as his hand snakes up my thigh. "We will talk later. Right now, I must have you."

"Wait, I—"

He pulls back and gives me an angry look. "You would deny your husband?"

I've had enough of this. Prophecy or not, I won't be pushed into something I'm not ready for. I meet his eyes evenly. "Yes. I'd prefer us to know one another before we go any further, Alexander. Is this acceptable to you, or not? Because if it isn't, then I cannot be yours."

He blinks down at me as if he cannot believe what I've just said. "You really would deny a prince?"

I tip my chin up. "Yes."

He huffs and then levels a dark glare at me. "I had wanted to give you pleasure before I followed through with my plan, but now you've ruined it."

"Your plan? What are you talking about?"

An evil grin curls his lips, and I watch as his eyes turn from blue to glowing green. "You will not fulfill the prophecy. Not now. Not ever."

Fear trickles down my spine. "Who—who are you?"

"I am your death," he growls.

Panicked, I jerk my knee up, slamming it into his groin.

He doubles over, groaning in pain. It only takes him a moment to recover. His head snaps up to me, anger burning in his eyes. He snarls. "I would have made this painless for you, but now you will suffer."

He lunges for me, but I jump back then rush to the door. I jerk on the handle, but it's locked and won't budge. Fear tightens my chest, and I race for another door across the room. His footsteps echo loudly behind me as he gives chase.

I'm barely through the door when I feel something jerk on my dress. The sharp ripping of fabric fills the space as he tears my skirt. I slam the door shut, locking him out.

The prince pounds on the door, the wood groaning with each assault of his fists. "Open this door! Now!"

I've never been so afraid in my life. I'm locked in the cleansing room, and there is nothing here I can use as a weapon. What am I going to do?

I try to focus my thoughts, hoping I can reach out to my guards, but it's useless. I can't focus beyond my fear as the door begins to give under the prince's attack.

With a loud groan, the door creaks on its hinges, slamming inward. The prince rushes in, his eyes burning with rage.

"Please," I beg, throwing my arms up to shield me. "Please, don't do this."

He rushes forward. His large hand grips my hair as he pins me against the sink counter. I struggle, but he slams my face against the vanity. Shards of glass splinter and drop to the floor like tinkling glass as I stare at my reflection in the shattered mirror.

He spins me to face him. Wrapping his hands tight around my neck, he begins to squeeze.

I sink to the floor, and he follows me, tightening his grip as his cruel gaze holds mine. My lungs burn, starving for oxygen. I slap at his hands and face, struggling to break free of his deadly hold.

I don't want to die. Not like this.

A spike of panic goes straight through me as the edges of my vision begin to go dark. A reflection catches my eye off to the side, and I notice a large shard of glass on the floor from the broken mirror.

Desperate, I reach for it and grip it tightly in my palm. Warmth blooms across my skin and blood drips from my hand as the jagged edges dig into my flesh. In one swift movement, I draw the sharp glass across his neck, slicing it open.

His eyes go wide, and a choked gasp escapes him as he covers his throat with his hands, trying to stem the bleeding from his mortal wound. Blood streams down his front as he collapses over me. The scent of iron fills the air so strong I can taste it on my tongue. I nearly gag as my hands slip in the sticky, red substance as I struggle to push him off of my body.

I have to get out from under him. I have to leave this place; it's not safe. The prince himself tried to kill me. I cannot stay here.

CHAPTER 15

KAI

Devon points to the large balcony three floors up in the palace. "She is there. The prince took her to that room."

I know I shouldn't, but I want to make sure Ella is all right. I turn to him as I try to decide. "What are you waiting for?" His green eyes search mine. "Go check on her."

"Yes," Nyx adds. "Just a quick glance to make sure she is safe."

I clench my jaw. "We should have made her complete the seal with us. It would have strengthened our bond and allowed us to sense if she were in any danger."

Cash shakes his head. "She is a maiden. It would not have been right to take her first kiss just to seal our bonds to her. You know how humans are about such things."

"Yes," Finn says. "We can complete the bond after she has consummated her marriage to the prince."

They are right. With a heavy sigh, I lift my gaze to the window above. Soft light spills out onto the balcony, and I hope that because the room is still lit, I will be able to make a quick sweep of the interior then come back immediately. After all, I do not wish to see Ella mating the prince. The mere thought of it fills me with dread. I need to make sure she is well. That is all. I look to my bond brothers. "I will take a quick look and return immediately. "Stay here."

I don't wait for their response as I take off.

As I fly up toward the balcony, a terrified scream rings out. My heart stops, then begins pounding. Furiously, I flap my wings. When I reach the window, I see the prince atop Ella. Her face bloodied and bruised as she struggles beneath him while he strangles her.

Rage burns through me like fire as I shift instantly and break through the window. The world shifts into slow motion as the glass shatters inward and I race toward her. Fear grips me in an iron vise as she cries out again. I cannot reach her fast enough.

Broken mirror pieces lay scattered on the floor all around them, crunching under her body as she wrestles beneath his larger form. She grips a large shard on the floor beside her. In one swift movement, she draws the sharp edge across his neck, slicing it open.

Blood gushes from his body as he collapses atop her.

She pushes at him, her hands slipping on the sticky, red fluid as tears stream down her face.

I grip his shoulder and roll him off of her, lifting her to her feet. Panic stops my heart as my gaze travels over her form. She's covered in blood. "Ella." I cup her cheek, drawing her attention to me and away from the gruesome display on the ground. Her eyes are wide as she stares up at me in shock. "Where are you hurt? Please, tell me."

"I'm fine," she barely manages, but I know she is not.

A broken sob escapes her. I grab her wrist and study her palm, noting the cuts from the glass. I tear a strip from her dress and quickly wrap it around her hand to stop the bleeding.

I gather her in my arms. "Ella!" I speak her name urgently as I gently cup her face and tip it toward me.

Her beautiful face is battered and bruised. Blood covers almost her entire body, and I'm scared because I do not know how much of it is hers. She trembles against me, sobbing heavily as tears stream down her face.

"What happened, Ella? Please, tell me. Where else are you injured?"

I trace my hands over her form, checking her for any wounds.

She shakes her head. "He tried to choke me, and I—" Her voice catches, and she curls further into me.

I hold her shaking form close to my chest, running my hand soothingly down her hair and back. Her dress is rumpled and torn in several places. My gaze drifts to the prince's lifeless form. "Ella," I whisper. "We have to get out of here."

I look back at his body, and my jaw drops when I observe it morph into the form of another man entirely.

Ella gasps beside me. "I—I don't understand. How did—"

"A wolf shifter." I study his face. He looks familiar but I cannot quite place how I know him. "They are the only ones of our kind who can change not only from human to beast. They can alter their human appearance to mimic the form of another human."

Her eyes are wide as they meet mine. "Then, where is the prince?"

"I do not know." I dart a glance toward the door. "But we must leave now."

She nods, and I quickly move us to the balcony. I glance down at my bond brothers. Their eyes are full of alarm as they notice Ella's disheveled state and the blood that covers her from head to toe.

"What happened?" Finn's voice cries out in my head.

"There is no time to explain. We must get her away from here. Quickly. I'm coming down."

I wrap my arms tightly around Ella's smaller form. As a shifter, we are able to partially transform, thus keeping the size of our human form while also retaining some of our animal attributes. For me, I'm able to use my wings, but it takes great concentration to do this. "Hold on to me, Ella. I'm going to fly us down."

She nods again and then climbs onto my front, wrapping her legs around my waist and her arms around my neck.

I move us toward the edge of the balcony and partially shift. Extending my wings, I walk off the ledge and glide gently to the ground.

Each of my brothers stares at us with wide eyes full of concern. *"What happened?"*

I shake my head. *"There is no time. I will explain everything later."* I look to Devon. *"Can you partially shift?"*

He nods and closes his eyes in concentration. Slowly, he transforms into a cat but much larger. Big enough that he can easily carry Ella on his back.

Still in shock, she clings tightly to me. I cup her chin and lift her tear-filled eyes to mine. "Ella, Devon is going to carry you. Can you hold on to him?"

"Yes," she mumbles, shaking.

Carefully, I place her on his back, guiding her arms around Devon's neck.

"Will you make it to the cottage?"

He growls as if offended I would ask such a thing and takes off from the castle as we follow closely behind.

The rest of us race away from the palace in our human forms. Everyone begins rapid-firing questions at me.

"What happened?" Nyx asks.

Finn looks to me. *"Why is she covered in blood?"*

I growl low in my throat as I send them the image of what I found when I reached the balcony window. "A wolf shifter took the form of the prince. He beat her, and she killed him."

"A wolf shifter?" Cash's voice rings out. *"I don't understand."*

"In the forest," Finn says. *"When we first found her. It was a wolf shifter who attacked. This is the second time a wolf shifter has attacked her within a few days. It is not a coincidence. Someone specifically is targeting her."* He looks to Nyx. *"Your dream was a warning. I believe they may have been sent by the Wolf Queen. Why else would two of them attack? They would not do this without the blessing of their pack leader."*

I grit my teeth. *"We will hide her away from both the humans and shifters. We must trust no one until we know for sure who was behind these attacks."*

CHAPTER 16

NYX

F inn's words unnerve me. He is right. I think of my recurring nightmares—the ones where the Wolf Queen kills Ella. She and her pack rule our kingdom. If they are after Ella, nowhere is safe for her. This is precisely what I've feared for so long. But why would they want to harm the Chosen One? It does not make sense. Why wouldn't the queen want peace between our two worlds?

Although it is difficult, I force myself to push these thoughts aside. Right now, we need to hide Ella; take her somewhere that no one can find her. And to do that, we will have to break one of our most sacred laws. We must bring a human across the veil and to our world.

It doesn't take long to reach the veil to our kingdom. As we pass through, the magic that keeps our lands hidden from the humans shimmers softly. I scan the forest for any sign that anyone notices the precious burden Devon carries upon his back. But no one is around. The sentries must have ignored our entry.

When we reach the cottage, I stop while everyone else continues ahead. I shift into my human form and begin weaving the spell that will shield us from unwanted eyes. It is an illusion of the strongest magic. No one is more skilled at illusory spells, in our group, than me. I will make certain no one can find us here. We'll keep Ella safe both from the humans and others of our kind.

We built this cottage based on a premonition from one of my dreams many years ago. I dreamed of danger, but I did not know what form it would take, nor the context in which it might arrive. I only knew that we would need someplace hidden; a safe place to shelter from unwanted eyes.

It says much about Kai that he trusted me enough to act on my dream. And now the day has arrived that I've long dreaded. All our lives are in danger.

The penalty for bringing a human across the veil is imprisonment and death. I've no desire to face either, but keeping Ella safe is worth the risk. She is precious, cherished, and treasured beyond all measure. I know that my bond brothers feel the same as me.

Once finished, I start back for the cottage. It sits in a clearing deep in the forest. Tall trees surround us like a giant wall on all sides. Constructed of gray stone with a thatched roof, it appears much smaller on the outside than it actually is. I layered several illusory spells throughout the structure to achieve this effect. It looks as though it is only one level and could contain, at most, two rooms. Inside it is rather palatial, and I hope Ella finds it pleasing.

I walk inside to find Kai and Devon standing in the living area. "Where is—" I begin to ask, but Kai interrupts.

"Cash and Finn have drawn her a bath. They are with her now. Of all of us, she is closest to them, so I thought it best that they stay there with her."

I sigh, knowing she is in good hands. Normally, I would be jealous, but not now, not after what happened.

CHAPTER 17

ELLA

W e're so deep in the forest, I'm not sure I'd ever be able to find my way out of here by myself. It felt like we ran for such a long time after we left the castle and crossed the veil into the shifter kingdom.

A small burst of warmth traveled over my skin as we entered the magical barrier. I thought Kai said it was forbidden for them to bring me here, but I suppose they didn't have a choice.

I'm worried though for their safety. I hate that they're having to risk so much just for me.

Cash and Finn help me down off Devon's back. It's so strange that he and Kai are able to partially shift into a larger form than usual. I wonder if all of them have this ability.

Unbidden memories resurface as I recall my attack. Tears fill my eyes, but I blink them back, trying to appear much calmer than I feel in this moment. I could have died tonight. The thought hits me like a giant wave, and it takes everything

I have to keep it together. I don't want to break down and start crying. I'm stronger than that.

Cash gathers me in his arms and carries me toward the entrance to a small cottage. It sits in the middle of a clearing, surrounded by a dense forest full of trees taller than any I've ever seen in the human kingdom. Great trees stretch up toward the sky, majestic and heavily laden with thick branches full of green needle-like leaves. There are so many that they form a wall between this place and the outside world.

The cottage itself seems relatively small in comparison. Gray stone walls and a straw-thatched roof with small windows and one door in the front. It looks as if it will hold no more than two people comfortably, so I don't know how all of us are going to stay here.

When we move inside, my jaw drops as I take in the massive space. It seems this place is full of magic to appear so tiny outside compared to what it actually is. Tall ceilings with large wooden beams span the entire length of the room. A massive fireplace against the far wall has a large gray sofa and table before it. Several plush gray rugs cover the smooth stone floors. I marvel at the intricate carvings in both the furnishings and the baseboards. Nature scenes and winding vines etched into the wood that appear so real they're beautiful.

The living area opens up into a large kitchen with a long counter that overlooks the living space. Cash takes me up a winding staircase to the second floor.

It opens up into a bedroom with one massive bed in the center that will most definitely accommodate everyone. The fireplace beside it is not as large as the one downstairs, but it is still rather impressive and stacked with several thick cords of wood.

Cash walks to a door along the far wall and it opens up into a bathroom, complete with a large tub. He sets me down on a stool near the sink while he and Finn draw me a bath.

I turn to see my reflection in the mirror and gasp. I look terrible. The left side of my face is swollen and bruised. Bloodstains mark a gash across my cheek. My once beautiful dress is tattered, torn, and stained red, barely covering my breasts from where the wolf shifter ripped it as we struggled.

The dark memories of my assault resurface, and I draw in a shaking breath as fresh tears escape my lashes and roll softly down my face.

Finn gathers me in his arms and pulls me close to his chest. "You're safe now, Ella. No one will harm you here. My vow."

I nod against him, but I cannot speak. He cups my cheek and his warm green gaze meets mine. "Do you want me to help you undress?"

I tense, and his eyes fill with pain. Cash moves to his side. "We will not touch you in any way that makes you uncomfortable, Ella. We simply want to take care of you."

I nod, ashamed that I would have such a reaction to him. They took care of me before without pushing themselves on me. I trust them.

Carefully, they undo the bindings of my dress and slip it from my shoulders as they guide me to the tub. Steam rises from the surface, and as I sink deep into the warm water, I feel my muscles beginning to unwind and relax.

Finn gently washes my hair as Cash runs a soft cloth over my face, neck, and shoulders, cleaning away all the blood.

"You are very brave, Ella," Cash says.

Numbly, I stare at the water, watching as the clear liquid slowly turns pink from all the blood on my skin. I shudder inwardly. "I don't feel very brave right now," I murmur. "I know he's dead, but…" I clench my jaw as I swallow against the hard lump in my throat. "I'm still afraid." I look to Finn. "What if someone followed us here? What if they come after all of you too?"

Finn takes my hand. "We made certain no one followed us. We are safe here."

I want so much to believe this. But if the wolf shifter that attacked me took the form of the prince, that means that he and whoever he's working with were able to either kill or abduct the prince before that.

And if they can get to a prince—a man surrounded by royal guards and safe in his castle—they can get to anyone. None of us are truly safe.

I don't point this out, however, because it will do no good. We have nowhere else to go.

Cash and Finn help me stand and wrap me in a soft, warm towel to dry. Cash hands me a nightgown. The light blue material is smooth as silk against my skin. It's held up by two small straps over my shoulders and only goes down to mid-thigh.

Usually, I would feel shy about wearing something so revealing, but ever since I've met my guards, they have done nothing but protect and take care of me. I feel neither ashamed nor embarrassed to dress in front of them now.

I know it's only been a few days that I've known them, but it feels like it's been a lifetime. I suppose it's the bond that causes me to feel this way, but I don't care. My guards care for me and would never hurt me. That's all that matters.

Nyx comes up the stairs and walks toward us. He holds out a small tin, and I stare down at it curiously. "It is healing balm." His warm honey-brown eyes meet mine as he hands me the container. "Magically enhanced. It will heal your injuries."

I thank him, and he looks to Cash and Finn. "The rest of us will be downstairs. You two stay here."

"We will," Finn replies.

As he turns to leave, I grip his forearm, stopping him abruptly.

He spins back to me with a curious expression.

"Please," I whisper. "Be careful."

A warm smile crests his lips. "I will," he murmurs. "Rest, Ella. We will keep watch while you sleep."

Sleep. As if that's possible after everything that happened this night.

"Thank you," I barely manage.

As soon as he's gone, Cash takes the small tin from me and opens it. Tenderly, he applies the ointment to my cheek, and I release a sigh of relief as the pain fades then disappears completely. I walk back to the bathroom mirror, marveling at how I'm now completely healed.

I smooth my hand across my cheek as Cash moves up behind me. "Is the pain gone?"

"Yes. I don't hurt at all anymore. How does that work? I don't understand. And... where are we? Is this your home?"

Finn moves up beside him. "We brought you back to our kingdom."

I search his eyes in concern. "I thought Kai said it was forbidden for you to bring a human to your world. Aren't you going to get in trouble for bringing me here?"

"Not unless someone finds out." Finn lowers his gaze as he continues to concentrate on spreading the balm across my back from where small shards of glass cut my skin. "But no one will know, and no one will find you here."

"How do you know?" I peer over my shoulder, unable to fathom why they would take such a risk.

"Because we have hidden this place with an enchantment,

shielding it from unwanted eyes." Finn explains. "As long as we keep the shield up, no one will be able to find us."

"And no one but us knows about this place either," Cash adds. "We built it many years ago, shortly after we bonded. A sort of... escape for us, you see. A place to get away when we wanted to be alone."

I study him a moment. "You say you are all bond brothers, but what does that mean exactly?"

"It means," Finn begins. "That we are all bound to each other. We are a unit—able to speak to each other with our minds and thoughts. We are as close as brothers." His lips quirk up in a smile as he looks to Cash. "Perhaps even closer since we know so much about each other."

"But how were you all brought together?" I ask, curious to understand.

Cash holds out his arm, pointing to a glowing mark on his forearm. As I stare at it, it begins to glow even brighter. Finn steps forward and extends his arm as well, and I note that he has the same marking.

"This mark, "Cash gestures to it. "Each of us was born with it. It is the mark of the Chosen One." His eyes snap up to meet mine. "We were destined from birth to be your guards, Ella. We have trained our entire lives for this purpose."

"What does that mean?"

Finn looks to me. "It means that we were taken from our families when we were children and sent to live in a training house among the Elders so they could teach us about the prophecy and also how to guard you."

My heart clenches. "You were all taken from your families?"

"Yes," Finn replies. "But we still were allowed to see them from time to time."

I reach out and take his hand, squeezing it gently. "I'm so sorry. You gave up so much for me."

He shakes his head as he looks to his brother. "Do not be sad for us, Ella. Cash and I had each other and the rest... we are close as brothers. They are our family. And now you are as well. We are bound to you, just as we are bound to one another in an unbreakable bond."

Cash cups my cheek. "All my life, I dreamed of what it would be like to finally meet you. And now that we have, I know that you are brave and kind, intelligent and beautiful, Ella. I am honored to be your guard. I will protect you with my life if necessary."

"I will as well," Finn adds. "All of us would."

Cash stares down at me with a pained expression. "When Finn and I were growing up, no one could tell us apart. Even our bond brothers and our parents have difficulty with this." He sighs heavily. "At first, we thought of it as a game."

A faint smile curves Finn's lips. "It was fun until the day we realized that even the people we knew best could not tell us apart."

Cash glances at Finn, then turns his attention back to me. "We even met another female shifter of our kind. She was quite taken with me. Or so she claimed. But I wanted to know if her feelings were true before I allowed myself to fall. So, I told her that I was not interested but that my brother, Finn, was."

"What happened?" I ask.

Cash's eyes fill with sadness. "She said one was just as good as the other and had no qualms about going after Finn at that point."

Finn places a hand on Cash's shoulder. "I love my brother, but it has been... difficult for us because of this. Almost no one considers us as our own person. We are simply Cash and Finn—instead of being considered separately."

Still holding Finn's hand, I reach for Cash's as well. I look at Finn. "You are Finn, and you," I look to Cash, "are Cash."

They both smile down at me. Finn presses a tender kiss to my hand. "You are the only one who has always been able to tell. Even on the first day you met us. Even the Elders could not tell us apart half the time."

"Who are the Elders?" I ask for they keep mentioning them without any further explanation.

Cash answers. "They are the ones who interpret the ancient scrolls—prophecies written hundreds of years ago. They are written almost like riddles—difficult to interpret. But one thing is certain: the Chosen One's prophecy is that she will unite the two kingdoms. The human and shifter kingdom will become one because of her influence and relationship with the human prince."

I think back on the wolf shifter disguised as my supposed future husband. "The prince is probably already dead. How are we supposed to fulfill the prophecy now?"

"You are alive," Finn says. "You are the key. Whatever happens otherwise is nowhere near as important as that. That is why we must keep you safe. You are to unite our two kingdoms."

A tear slips down my cheek. "So, who are you going to try to marry me off to now?" I ask bitterly, remembering all that I just went through.

The wolf shifter was my first kiss, the first man ever to touch me so intimately. I wrap my arms around myself as I think back on it. I hate that this happened to me.

Finn pulls me into his arms and smooths his hand down my back. "Forgive us, Ella. It was our fault for leading you to him. We thought—" his voice catches. "We thought you would be happy with him. We did not know he wasn't the prince. I'm sorry."

Tears prick my eyes. "But how could you just give me

away to someone else like that?" I take his hand in mine and place it directly over my heart. "Do you not feel something between us? Because I do. I feel it here, in my heart."

I turn to Cash and take his hand as well. "I feel it for both of you. And I know it is wrong to feel this way for two men, but I cannot help it. And perhaps it's too early to say it is love... but, if it is not, I don't know what else it may be, because I have never felt it before the two of you."

Finn and Cash share a glance then look down at me, their green eyes studying me intently. "You love us, Ella?"

"Yes," my voice quavers. "And the entire time I was with the prin—" my voice hitches. "I mean the wolf shifter," I correct myself. "All I could think of was you and Cash."

Cash cups my cheek. "I must tell you something, Ella. The Elders warned us that the bonds would make us feel strongly toward you. And that you would feel strongly for us in return. What you are feeling may be a result of this and not—"

I press a finger to his lips to silence him. "Even if it is the bond, I don't care. If what you're saying is true and we are all bound to each other, then this feeling will remain, will it not?"

He nods.

Finn's eyes meet mine. "I cannot deny that I have been drawn to you from the first moment I saw you." He looks to Cash. "I'm certain my brother felt the same too. The Elders warned us of this. The pull of the bond is strong and it will only grow stronger once it is sealed. But we do not want to pressure you, Ella."

"But what if I want you as well?" I ask. "Do my feelings not matter?"

"Of course, they do," Finn protests. "But this is all new for you. We do not want you to make any decisions you might regret later."

Perhaps he is right, but in my heart, I do not feel this way. My heart insists that I love them. And I don't care if it's the bond that has made my feelings blossom so quickly. I've never felt this way for another. I lift my eyes to them. "You do not care that I have feelings for you both?"

A gentle smile curls Finn's lips. "No."

"Do shifters marry humans?" I ask because if they do, I have never heard of this before. After all, only a few days ago, I believed shifters were only myths.

Finn's expression falls into a look of sadness. "It is forbidden for a shifter to mate a human."

"Forbidden," the word leaves my lips in a hushed whisper. I could have died this night and all I could think of was my guards.

It's obvious Finn and Cash care for me as much as I do them. But even as I consider this, I know deep in my heart that it is more than that. I love them. Both of them. And I do not care if such a thing is forbidden. People are trying to kill me. Why not grab what happiness I can... while I am still alive?

We move to the bedroom, and Finn starts a fire while Cash tucks me under the blankets in the bed.

He sits on the edge, and Finn comes to join him. His warm green eyes search mine a moment before he reaches across and brushes the hair back from my face and tucks it behind my ear.

"Sleep, Ella," Finn whispers softly. "We will keep watch over you."

I place my hand over his. "Will you—" I bite my lip as warmth creeps up my neck to my cheeks.

"What is it?"

"Will you hold me?" I glance to Cash as well. "Both you? Like you did when we slept in my tower on the estate?"

"Are you sure you wish for us to lie beside you, Ella?" Finn asks, his gaze searching mine in concern.

"Yes," I mutter, already feeling the hidden weight of the day lift from my shoulders. "I feel... safe with you both."

But that is not the only reason. It is also because I could have been murdered and never felt the warmth of their arms around me again.

Finn crawls in beside me, and I turn into his arms, hugging him tightly. Cash lies down behind me, holding me close. I love being held by both of them. It makes me feel safe and loved.

Finn gently strokes my hair while Cash runs his hand soothingly up and down my hip. I tilt my head up to look at Finn. Tenderly, he skims the tip of his nose alongside mine. With his eyes closed, a deep rumbling purr vibrates from his chest. The soothing sound lulling me into a state of relaxation.

"Kai said the bond between us could be sealed with a kiss," I whisper.

His eyes snap open. "Yes. That is how it is done. The permanent binding of a female to her guards. But you do not need to decide this now, Ella."

"What if I've already decided?"

He stills and so does Cash behind me. His gaze holds mine. "You have been through much this night, Ella." He presses a soft kiss to my forehead. "Rest. You are safe. You do not need to permanently bind us to remain so. We are already bound to you of our own accord."

Everything inside me wants to cement the permanent bond with them. To seal them to me with a kiss. In my heart, I know what I feel is love, but I cannot silence the doubt in the back of my mind that insists this could all be the bond. So much has happened and I know enough of trauma, from all my years of abuse at the hands of my stepmother, that making rash decisions rarely turns out well.

So, instead of arguing that I am ready to seal them to me, I snuggle in between Cash and Finn, enjoying their warmth and safety. I think on their words. They claim we are safe here. Closing my eyes, I force myself to relax. And after what feels like an eternity, I begin to drift away into the oblivion of precious sleep.

CHAPTER 18

ELLA

When I wake, it's with a renewed sense of purpose. Morning light filters in through the window, casting a soft warm glow throughout the room. I stretch my body out between Cash and Finn. Finn's arms tighten around my waist as I do so.

To be honest, I love this feeling of sleeping between them. Just as I loved it back at the estate when they all slept around me at night. But the events of yesterday have caused everything to come into sharp focus with sparkling clarity.

For the first time, I'm waking up somewhere outside of my tower and away from my stepmother's cruelty. But the danger I used to face from her is far less than the one I must contend with now. Someone wants to kill me. Wolf shifters, specifically.

As my gaze travels over the room, it occurs to me that I've traded one cage for another. I cannot leave this place. Not until it is truly safe and no one is coming after me. Having this small taste of freedom away from my cruel stepmother has strengthened my resolve to live.

But that's the problem. I don't want to just survive, I want to truly be free. And in order to do that, I need to understand more about this world and the prophecy. If the prince is as key to all of this as I am, I have to find out what happened to him.

I sit up in bed.

Finn and Cash sit up with me, each of them staring at me in concern. "Are you all right?" Finn smooths a hand down my arm. "Are you hungry?"

I nod.

After I shower and dress, I come out from the cleansing room. Finn's eyes meet mine and I'm so grateful for them, my heart could burst. They were right to insist that I rest and not make any decisions last night.

I would not have regretted sealing them to me. Not in the slightest. But because I did not, it affords me the opportunity to lay everything out. If they are to be my guards and protect me, I want to make sure it happens on my terms. I refuse to allow a prophecy to dictate my life. For the first time in all my years of suffering under the cruel hand of fate, I've decided to take control of my life.

When we walk downstairs, Kai, Nyx, and Devon are already waiting. A table has already been laid out with plates of food for breakfast.

I take a seat at the head of the long rectangular table and my gaze travels over the selection.

"We made a bit of everything," Nyx says. "We were uncertain what you might prefer this morning."

Honeyed cakes, fresh fruit, toast, eggs. I've never seen

such a feast. Not even at the estate. "How did you manage all of this?" I ask.

"Magic has many uses," Nyx explains. "We have been storing food here for several years. In case we had use of this place. Magic kept everything in stasis, waiting to be used at the timing of our choice."

I look to him. "Cash and Finn said you built this place many years ago. Why?"

"I had a dream," Nyx explains. "That someday we would be in danger. That we'd need a place to hide. So…" His eyes sweep to Kai. "I spoke of this to Kai and we decided to act upon that information."

My mouth drifts open. "You are a seer?"

He shrugs. "Of sorts. I often have visions of the future in my dreams."

I lean forward. "And what about now? Do you know what happened to the prince? Or who is after me?"

He lowers his gaze. "The prince… I do not know what happened to him. But as far as who seeks to harm you… I believe it is the Wolf Queen. She is the ruler of the Shifter Kingdom."

"Why would she want me dead?"

Although I'm looking to Nyx, it's Kai that answers. "I believe it is because she may see you as a threat to her power. The prophecy states you will unite the two kingdoms. You and the prince. Perhaps it may also mean that you will rule over both as well. And this, she would not want." He pauses. "We must find a way to secure your safety while—"

"I'll not be married off to someone else," I state firmly.

Kai blinks at me in confusion. "I… that's not what I was going to suggest."

I clench my jaw as anger sweeps through me. "And yet you were the one who convinced me to trust in the prophecy. You would have given me over to the prince because of some words in an ancient text." I shake my head. "I won't be used like that. Not anymore."

His blue eyes are full of pain as his gaze holds mine. "Forgive me, Ella. I—"

I stand from the table. "We're going to find the prince. And if he's alive, we will rescue him and restore him to his throne. But I will not marry him just because of some prophecy. I will do whatever must be done to bring peace between the kingdoms. If that is what I am supposed to do, it will be done on my terms." I meet Kai's eyes evenly. "I won't be a pawn of fate. Not anymore and not ever again."

With that, I walk to the door and out into the clearing. The sun is shining brightly overhead as I make my way toward the tree line. My heart hammers in my chest as I struggle to push down the maelstrom of emotions deep within. After so many years of having to hide away my true feelings, it's difficult to allow them to surface now.

It's as if all the years of pent-up frustration and anger are roiling inside me, threatening to spill over. I don't want to be angry though. I just want to be heard. For the first time, I will be the one to decide my fate. I won't have anyone dictate it for me.

Footsteps behind me, draw my attention and I turn to find Kai on my heels. "Ella," he calls out. "Wait."

I spin to face him, waiting for him to catch up.

He blinks down at me, his eyes full of worry. "You are angry at me."

Kai says this as a statement, but I know it is also a question. "Yes."

Before he can speak, I begin. "I heard you, Kai. In the carriage on the way to the ball." I pause, trying to push down my emotions before I continue. "When you spoke in their minds and you thought I couldn't hear." Tears sting my eyes, but I blink them back. "You all have feelings for me. Just as I do for each of you. You made them all agree to ignore them. Told them that all they could be to me were my guards."

"It is an effect of the bond," he says. "It—"

"I don't care," I snap. "Even if it is, it feels real enough to me. And I know from what you said to the others that you each feel the same way too. And yet—" my voice catches, and a tear slips down my cheek. I quickly brush it away. "You were just going to give me away. Hand me over to some other man just because of some prophecy that you don't even entirely understand."

Kai reaches for me, but I step back.

He gives me a pained look. "Do you hate me?"

"No. I'm angry, but I don't hate you. I'm to blame as well because I was just blindly going to go along with the plan, even though it felt wrong from the beginning." I draw in a deep and steeling breath. "But no more. We have to find the prince. If he is the key to fulfilling this prophecy of peace, we need him. But I won't marry him just to secure this. I refuse."

I look over his shoulder to the others, allowing my gaze to sweep over each of them. My eyes land on Nyx. "Tell me more about your dreams and about the prophecy. If this is going to work, I need to understand everything."

CHAPTER 19

KAI

A terrible ache settles deep in my chest as Ella walks away from me and toward Nyx. His brown eyes dart to me and I dip my chin in a subtle nod. She wants to learn from him. Not me. I have lost her trust.

She is right. I would have given her over to the prince simply because it is what I've been told we should do. The Elders ingrained this mission in our minds from the time we were young. I thought I was doing the right thing, but it is clear to me now that I was not.

I believed that giving her to the prince was a sacrifice *I* was having to make. It did not occur to me that it was a sacrifice on her part too. Ella is as brave as she is kind. Even despite her doubts, she would have gone through with marrying the prince because she trusted us. She trusted *me*. And I let her down. I delivered her into danger, and she could have died because of it.

Cash and Finn walk toward me, concern evident in their features. Devon places a hand on my shoulder. "Are you—"

I shrug him off. "I'm fine. I will fly the perimeter and make certain no one is nearby."

Before they can answer, I shift into my blue jay form and take flight.

CHAPTER 20

ELLA

Nyx explains the details of his dreams to me. How he saw the Wolf Queen kill me in his visions.

I meet his gaze evenly. "Are your dreams always right?"

"No. Sometimes, they are just dreams." He hesitates. "But two wolf shifters have tried to kill you. That has to be more than just coincidence."

"How do we find out if she's behind it?"

"I believe that for now, we should stay here. We must wait and see what the Wolf Queen does."

"Why?"

"You have escaped two of her assassins. If she is behind this, she will search for you now that you have gotten away. Either way, whoever was responsible for the attempts on your life will not have given up so easily. We must wait to see who comes after you."

I shake my head. "What if I don't want to wait? What if

we go to a neighboring kingdom? I could hide there. Start a new life."

He takes my hand and gives me a pitying look. His warm, honey-brown eyes staring deep into mine. "It is not that simple, Ella. Whoever is after you, they believe in the prophecy and they seek to prevent it from happening. They will not rest until you are no longer a threat."

Despite my fear, I meet his gaze evenly. "Fine. We will wait."

When Nyx and I return to the cottage, Cash and Finn are already inside. They greet me with a warm smile as soon as I enter, and I return it in kind. Of all my guards, they are the ones I feel closest to. Perhaps it's because they found me first, or maybe it's just their personalities. I'm not sure, but I don't question it any further.

I already have enough uncertainty in my life at the moment.

They offer me a plate of food since I left before I ate any breakfast earlier. I eagerly take it from them and sit at the table.

I glance over at the living area. "Where are Kai and Devon?"

Cash answers. "They are patrolling the perimeter."

He looks to Nyx and something unspoken passes between them, but I do not ask what it is. Instead, I lean forward. "I want you to teach me to fight."

Finn blinks down at me. "You have us. We are your guards. You do not need to—"

"Yes, I do." I look to each of them. "I was the one who had to fend off the wolf shifter last night. It was luck that I was able to kill him. He could just as easily have killed me instead."

Finn's warm green eyes stare deep into mine. "You are right. We failed you. Forgive us, Ella."

I shake my head softly. "You did not fail me. I just… I would feel better if I were able to defend myself. In case I am alone again with… an attacker."

His eyes sweep to Nyx. "Nyx is the one who should train you. He is the one who learned fastest when we were younger. He helped each of us to master our skills."

Nyx dips his chin in acknowledgement and then turns to me. "We will start tomorrow if you wish."

"Why not now?"

He cocks his head to the side to regard me. "You were injured yesterday. Your body is still healing."

He's right. "Tomorrow, then."

"Tomorrow," he confirms. "In the meantime, I believe you would benefit from more healing balm."

"I'm fine. It already—"

"Your skin has knitted back together where your wounds once were, but the muscles beneath would benefit from the healing properties of the salve even now."

He gives me another tin of healing cream and I walk upstairs to the bedroom. Cash and Finn follow silently behind me, and I'm glad for their company. Nyx's words replay in my mind. I shudder inwardly as I think on the fact that someone wants me dead.

I turn back to Cash and Finn and make a decision. Nothing is certain. I could be killed tomorrow. I've decided that I'm going to live my life how I choose. And that means taking whatever happiness I can, and denying my heart no more.

CHAPTER 21

ELLA

I take a warm bath and then allow Cash and Finn to apply the healing balm over my skin. It carries the delicate fragrance of honey and jasmine and feels like silk as they spread it over my flesh.

When they're finished, I lay down in the bed and they lay on either side of me like before. Finn in front and Cash behind me. Each of them with an arm around my waist.

"Are you tired, Ella?" Finn asks.

I shake my head. I reach out and cup Finn's cheek. In my heart, I already know that I love him and his brother, but I need to know if they truly feel the same in return. "You told me last night that you have strong feelings, but... do you love me?"

"Yes," Finn replies without hesitation.

I search his eyes. "Then how could you just stand by and offer me up to another man? How could you send me into the arms of the prince? I understand why Kai did it. He thought it was his duty as your leader to make sure the prophecy was fulfilled. But you?" I turn and look back at Cash as well. "Why did you both go along with it?"

Finn clenches his jaw. "Because I thought he would give you the kind of future you deserve. One full of love and happiness and—"

I press a finger to his lips to silence him. "Are you saying you couldn't give this to me as well?"

He looks to his brother, an uncertainty in his gaze. I roll onto my back to stare up at Cash. He reaches down and touches my cheek. "All of us love you," he says. "But we thought the prince would give you a life that we never could. One of wealth and—"

I give him an incredulous look. "What do riches matter to the heart? Love and happiness are more precious than all the gold in the world."

"It is forbidden for a shifter to take a human mate," Finn says. "We would have to hide you from both our world and yours." He pauses. "And the Elders told us you were the Chosen One. The one who must marry the prince and bring peace to both of our realms."

"They were wrong," I snap. Blinking back tears, I turn onto my side and hug my knees to my chest as I swallow back a sob. "Even if the prince is not dead, I refuse to be passed off like—" My voice breaks, and I stop abruptly as the first tear escapes my lashes.

Finn pulls me into his arms and gently strokes my cheek. "Ella, I am so sorry. We all are. If we had known, we would never have left you alone with him. Forgive us, please."

"Promise me you'll never try to give me away to someone else," I murmur against his chest. "I don't want to go with anyone but all of you. I refuse. You are the only ones I feel safe with. You are the only ones I love. No one else."

He stills. "What are you saying, Ella?"

"I'm saying that I love you, Finn. I love you and Cash. And

I know it's wrong to love more than one person, but I can't help it. That's how I feel. And even if it's the bond making me feel like this… it doesn't matter." I place my hand to my chest, directly over my heart. "I feel it in here. But I feel it for you both. Is that wrong?"

Finn's gaze holds mine as he threads his fingers through my hair. "It is not wrong in our world to love more than one person."

"In fact," Cash adds, "it is not unheard of for a female to mate each of her guards."

"It isn't?" I ask as hope fills me.

"No," he replies. "It is only you humans who believe it is wrong to take more than one mate."

I draw in a shaking breath as the horrible memory returns of the wolf shifter disguised as the prince. "When I was with him, it felt wrong," I whisper, recalling what went through me while I was at the castle. "It felt wrong because I knew that I wanted you. Both of you. But I thought you wouldn't want me, especially since you had done everything to make sure that he noticed me. That he picked me and—" my voice catches.

Finn pulls me tight to his chest as Cash wraps his arms around me as well, holding me between them.

"If you loved me, how could you just give me away to someone else?"

"You think I wanted to let you go?" Finn asks. He grips my chin and lifts my eyes to meet his. "It was the most difficult thing I have ever had to do. And when I saw you with him in the garden, I... I thought I would die of a broken heart. It was so hard to see you with him. And I knew... I knew that I would never want another as I want you. I love you, Ella. We both do."

"He's right," Cash murmurs, as he touches my cheek. "You

have ruined us for all other females. We are bound to you, heart, mind, body, and soul."

I turn onto my back. Each of them are propped up on one elbow. They stare down at me as I reach out for them. Gently, I stroke my hand up and down Finn's arm as I touch Cash's face. "Before he tried to kill me, the wolf shifter tried to seduce me. My first time would have been..." I blink back tears. "It would have been... not what I wanted. It felt wrong when he touched me. I want my first time to be special. And I want it on my terms." I pause, looking at both twins. "All I could think is that if given a chance, I would have been with one of you first instead of him."

Finn's eyes go half-lidded as I trail my hand down his bare chest. My fingers tracing every dip and curve of his heavily muscled form. I reach out and skim my fingers along Cash's bicep. The thick cords of muscle flexing beneath my touch.

I move my hand lower, and when I reach what should be the waistband of Finn's pants, I do not feel anything but his skin. My brow furrows in confusion as a smile tugs at his lips. "Our clothes are an illusion. Part of the form we take when we shift to make you feel comfortable," he explains.

He explained this before and I forgot that they are always naked, even when they appear to be clothed. My face heats as I stare up at them. "I want to see you," I whisper. "All of you."

I watch in wonder as their clothes fade away to reveal their completely nude forms.

Finn's gaze follows mine to his cock. I know I have seen it before when he was injured, but this is different. Now it is hard and fully erect and so much larger than I realized. My thighs involuntarily squeeze together as I wonder how he might feel inside me. "Forgive me, Ella," he whispers. "You are so beautiful I—"

I give him a quick kiss to silence him. "It's all right," I

whisper against his lips. When I look at Cash, his cock is hard and fully erect as well.

I wrap my hands around Finn's length. He is so large my fingers do not quite reach all the way around him. Liquid beads at the tip then runs down his shaft.

Breathless with anticipation, I look between them both. "Touch me," I command.

Cash smooths his hand up my thigh as Finn gently pushes the top strap of my gown off my shoulder. His intense green gaze holds mine as he cups my breast.

He leans down and closes his mouth over the soft peak, laving his tongue across it until it turns into a hard bead. I run my hand through his hair as I arch up against him, wanting more.

Cash's hand skims lightly up my inner thighs, but he stops just before he reaches my center. I want him to touch me so badly, I open my legs and stare deep into his eyes. A low moan escapes me as Finn continues to tease his tongue over my nipple and creates a gentle suction, driving me mad with desire.

"Touch me, Cash," I barely manage to breathe.

He stares at me with a heavy-lidded gaze as he dips his fingers into my already slick folds. I gasp as he brushes his thumb across the small bundle of nerves at the apex. He presses his lips to mine, swallowing the soft whimper of need that escapes me.

"May I taste you?" he asks, and I barely manage to nod as Finn moves his attention to my other breast.

Cash moves down between my thighs and runs his tongue through my folds. He concentrates on the small pearl of flesh at the top until I'm breathless and panting beneath them.

Finn lifts his head, and his green eyes meet mine. "I desire more than anything to be bound to you, Ella," he whispers. "I want to be yours." He cups my cheek. "Your kiss will seal us as your guards, but I... I want to be more than that. I want to be your mate, Ella." He darts a glance at Cash, his green eyes already watching me with a possessive gaze. "We both do."

"I want you," I barely manage to breathe. "Both of you. More than anything."

"You are certain?" Cash asks, hope shining in his eyes.

"Yes," I reply without hesitation.

"First, you must bind us as your guards with a kiss of intent."

"What does that mean?"

"You speak the words: I bind you as my guard," he explains. "Then you seal this vow with a kiss."

"And what about taking you as mine?" I ask because I want them both forever. I don't want the prince, and I don't care what the prophecy says. I want Cash and Finn as my mates.

Cash runs his fingers through my hair. "Are you certain you want us?"

I cup my hand to the back of his neck, pulling his mouth back down to mine. "I bind you as my guard," I whisper.

He captures my lips in a searing kiss and I gasp. When I open my mouth, his tongue finds mine, deepening our kiss.

"I love you, Ella," he whispers between kisses.

"I love you too, Cash."

Finn lifts his head, and his eyes meet mine full of uncertainty.

I smile down at him. "I love you too, Finn."

He moves up my body and stares down at me with a look of intense love and devotion. I pull his mouth down to mine and seal him to me with a kiss.

Finn touches my cheek, staring down at me with an intense look of love and devotion. "If we mate with you, Ella, it will bind us to you always as your mates. Do you want this?"

"Yes, I do."

Carefully, they both help to remove my gown. Once I'm bare before them, their eyes travel over my naked form, full of desire and hunger.

Finn moves over me. I open my thighs, and he settles between them. I look down my body and see the crown of his cock. Hard and erect, it is so large I'm not sure how he will fit inside me. As if sensing my concern, he cups my cheek. His green eyes stare down at me full of love. "I will go slow, Ella. But if it hurts, you must tell me, and we will stop."

"I trust you."

Anticipation moves through me as he fits himself to my entrance. His gaze holds mine and the breath stutters from my lungs as he slowly enters me. At first, everything is so tight it's uncomfortable. I dig my fingers into his arms as I try to force myself to relax. He stills. "Do you wish me to stop?" he asks, his voice rough and uneven.

"No," I tell him. "I want you."

He rocks his hips back and forth as he moves deeper. Cash closes his mouth over my breast, gently teasing the stiff peak. Small ripples of pleasure travel down my body to my core, and I begin to relax, adjusting to Finn's invasion as he slowly sheathes himself completely inside me. I wrap my legs around his hips, enjoying the sensation of being joined to him like this. I've never felt so full, and I love the way he stares down at me as if I were the most precious thing in the world to him.

Cash cups my breast with his other hand, and I turn to kiss him long and deep as Finn rolls his hips against mine.

The delicious friction of his length deep in my channel makes me moan. He stares down at me, his gaze fiery and possessive as he begins to stroke inside me.

Cash's tongue wraps around mine, stealing the breath from my lungs as Finn continues to move over me. Each stroke becomes longer, deeper, and more forceful. Heat builds deep within me as pleasure coils tight in my core.

A burst of heat deep inside me makes me gasp and arch up against him. It feels so good as it spreads throughout my body. My toes curl, and my eyelids flutter softly. "What was that?" I barely manage.

"My precum. It will soften the entrance to your womb to receive my essence," he says. "To seal the bond, your body must take in my seed."

Desire churns deep inside me. I want all of him. Everything he will give me. I look to Cash and know in my heart that I want them both. I want to bind myself to them.

Finn's eyes search mine. "Tell me that you are mine, my beautiful Ella."

"I'm yours."

He smiles and kisses me with a passion that steals the breath from my lungs as he thrusts up into me. Each stroke sends sensations so intense I'm gasping and panting his name.

Finn groans as I wrap my legs tighter around him. He changes the angle of his hips, sinking impossibly deeper inside me. A low growl rumbles in his chest.

He clenches his jaw, and I can tell it is taking everything in him to maintain his control. "Need you to come for me, Ella. Open for me and receive my essence, my beloved."

Cash closes his mouth over my breast as he cups the other one in his hand. The small muscles of my channel begin to flex and quiver around Finn's length before clamping down firmly.

My head falls back as waves of intense pleasure overcome me. I cry out Finn's name as the sensation ripples through my body. His cock pulses deep in my channel, and I'm flooded with a delicious warmth as he erupts inside me. He roars my name as he fills me with his essence. Heat blooms deep in my core. It feels as if it goes on forever, and I hold tightly to him, afraid to let go because it's so intense.

He collapses on top of me, and I love the feel of his body pressed against mine. But Cash's gaze is full of hunger as he stares down at me on his side. He touches his brother's shoulder and Finn pulls away from me.

I whimper softly at the loss of his cock from my body, but I only have a moment to miss him before Cash moves over me. He notches his tip at my entrance. His eyes meet mine, seeking permission. "Do you want me, Ella?" he rasps.

"Yes." I reach up and cup this cheek. "I want you, Cash."

My mouth falls open as he begins to push into me. He rocks his hips back and forth, moving deeper each time until he's fully seated inside me. Everything feels more sensitive now, and I gasp as he begins to move.

A soft moan escapes me at the delicious feel of his hardness rubbing my channel in all the right ways.

Finn cups my cheek and turns my head to face him. A moment later, he captures my mouth in a searing kiss as Cash continues to pump into me.

"You feel so good, Ella," Cash rasps. "You're perfect, my beautiful mate." His green eyes stare deep into mine with love and devotion. "Open yourself to me, Ella. Take my essence and bind us together."

I spread my hips a bit wider as he drives even deeper. He cups my backside to lift me from the bed as I wrap my legs around him. The angle of his hips makes everything that much more sensitive. I close my eyes as delicious sensations move through me with each thrust of his body deep into mine.

He grips my hip firmly in his hands, pinning me in place as he strokes long and deep, dragging me closer to the edge.

My body goes taut like a bowstring, and then I'm coming. My release roars through me so intense I cry out his name.

His cock pulses in my channel; heat blooms deep in my core as he floods my womb, filling me with his seed. Just like with Finn, it feels like it goes on forever.

When he pulls himself free of my body, I immediately miss the feel of him inside me. Finn moves over me, and as he gently parts my legs, I stare up at him in wonder. "Again?" I ask, stunned that he has recovered so quickly. I've overheard enough of the staff on the estate, before my stepmother let them go, to know that men require a refractory period before they can make love again, but it seems like this isn't the case for shifters.

Finn's eyes meet mine. "I have to have you again, my beautiful Ella. Do you want me?"

I cup his cheek and smile up at him. "Always."

CHAPTER 22

ELLA

When I wake in the morning, Cash and Finn have their arms wrapped tightly around me. I love being nestled between them. The area between my thighs aches, but in a good way, reminding me that I've been sealed and bound to them both.

As if sensing I'm awake, Finn's eyes slowly open, and he smiles at me.

Cash's lips caress my neck in a series of tender kisses as his hard length presses against my backside. I push back against him, loving the press of his body to mine.

"If you keep doing that," he whispers against the shell of my ear. "I'm going to have to take you."

I smile and push back again. "I want you inside me," I whisper, taking him up on his challenge.

He guides his length into me from behind. A low groan escapes him as he sheathes himself entirely inside me.

Finn's cock is hard against my abdomen, and I wrap my

hand around his length as he captures my mouth in a claiming kiss.

Cash grips my hips as he pumps into me, sending small ripples of pleasure through my entire body, and I begin to stroke Finn's shaft.

"Do you like the way I feel?" Finn asks as he cups his hand to my breast.

"Yes," I breathe against his lips. "I love holding you like this. That you trust me with the most vulnerable part of you just as I trust you when you enter my body."

He kisses me long and deep as he brushes his thumb across the peak of my breast. "You're perfect, Ella. Your body is so soft and giving." He closes his eyes. "I long to sink myself deep inside you again and fill you with my essence."

As he speaks, my inner walls clamp tightly around Cash's cock as he pumps into me. He grips my hips firmly to hold me in place. "Come for me, Ella," he breathes in my ear. "Open yourself and take all of me."

His words and the movement of his cock deep in my channel ignites a spark of pleasure in my core. It turns into a roaring flame when my release moves through me; he growls as he erupts deep inside me as we come together.

Finn's length twitches in my grasp, and a burst of warmth coats my abdomen. When Cash unsheathes himself from my body, Finn pulls me to him and enters me in one long stroke.

I cry out at the sensation as he begins to thrust. "You are perfect, Ella," he breathes against my lips as Cash continues to kiss along my neck, cupping my breasts from behind.

"Tell me you want me," he whispers.

"I want you, Finn. I want you," I breathe.

He clamps his hand on my thigh, holding me firmly to him as his strokes become deeper and more urgent.

The faster pace creates a delicious friction deep inside

me, pushing me over the edge. I open my mouth and cry out his name as wave after wave of pleasure moves through me.

He slams his hips against mine, and his cock begins to pulse. Warmth erupts from his body as he fills me again with his seed.

When he's finished, he remains inside me. Cash continues to press soft kisses to my neck and back while Finn skims his nose from my temple down to my jaw. "You are ours, Ella. And we'll always protect you," he whispers against my skin.

When he finally pulls away from my body, my thighs and abdomen are sticky with their release. Finn retrieves a towel from the bathroom and tenderly cleans me.

"I can take a bath," I offer.

Finn shakes his head and presses another kiss to my lips.

Cash cups my face, and I turn my head back to his so he can do the same. "No," he breathes into my mouth. "You smell of us." A low growl of arousal escapes his lips. "We prefer you this way." I moan as he cups my breast and kisses me deep. "You are ours, Ella. And we're never letting you go."

I stare deep into his eyes. "I never want to leave either of you. Ever again. I'm yours, and you are mine."

CHAPTER 23

NYX

As I stand in the kitchen preparing breakfast, I grit my teeth as I hear Finn growl upstairs and roar Ella's name. She cries out as well, and I am so jealous I can hardly stand it. I swear, the next time they shift, I'm going to rip those two chipmunks to shreds with my bare teeth.

I look to the living room and find Devon lounging lazily on the couch. I gesture angrily to him. "How can you just lie there like that? Do you not hear what's going on upstairs?"

His eyes snap open, and he stares directly at me. His green, vertically slit pupils narrowing. "Of course, I can hear it. I am trying to ignore it. You should do the same."

"How can I?" I snap. "They have been doing this all night and now this morning as well."

Kai walks in from outside. He looks between the two of us. "What is the problem here?"

Ella cries out, and his gaze lifts to the ceiling. He looks back at us with understanding and sighs heavily. "They are our brothers. We should not be jealous of them. We should be happy for them... and for her."

I arch a brow. "And what if she wants only them and not us as well?"

Kai clenches his jaw but says nothing. That tells me he is worried about it too. I feel sorry for him. He is the one who took the brunt of her anger yesterday. She is mad at him for trying to push her toward the prince just to fulfill the prophecy.

He is our leader, and it is because of this that she holds him more responsible than she does the rest of us. I pity my brother. It was easy to read the devastation in his blue eyes yesterday. And as I look to him now, the haunted expression has not left him this morning either.

Now he worries, just as Devon and I do, that she will not want us. She is human, and she may wish only to have two of us instead of all of us.

If that is the case, it will be difficult to watch my brothers so happy and in love with their mate while I remain alone and miserable. I cast a glance at Devon and Kai. Well, I suppose I will not be alone in my misery, so there's that.

It goes quiet upstairs, and I wonder if they are finally sleeping. They will probably remain up there the rest of the day since I am almost certain they did not get any rest at all last night.

I am surprised when I hear footsteps at the top of the stairs. I look up and find Ella wearing her nightshift and robe we procured for her. Her hair is tousled, and her clothing is rumpled, but despite her disheveled appearance, she is still the most beautiful female I have ever seen.

Cash and Finn walk beside her, and when they reach the kitchen, they take a seat on either side of her as Kai serves everyone breakfast.

It is difficult, but I manage to push down my jealousy as we eat.

Kai's gaze sweeps over us and lands upon me. "I know your illusion magic skills are strong. But the wolf shifters can see past certain spells due to their heightened sense of smell. I need you to make sure you fortify the shield you erected to hide us."

I nod. I had planned on weaving more spells into our cloak this morning anyway, for that specific reason.

Devon leans forward. "I do not understand. Why would the wolf shifters go against the prophecy? The Elders are the ones who assigned us to Ella so that she could unite the two kingdoms. Why would they not wish for peace among our two peoples?"

Kai shakes his head. "I do not know. Perhaps the Wolf Queen and her kin see Ella as a threat to her rule. I only know what I saw that night in the castle. The male who attacked Ella was not the prince. He must have possessed strong magic, indeed, to have hidden so well. None of us even detected that he was a shifter."

I have considered this. Our kind is always able to sense one another. To see past the human façade to the animal beneath. But with the prince, I detected nothing that night to indicate he was not entirely human.

I think again about my recurring nightmare of the Wolf Shifter Queen killing Ella. I turn to Kai. He is our leader, and from the look in his eyes, it is easy to see that he already has a plan. "What should we do?"

He meets my gaze evenly. "I will fly out to find one of the Elders. I must consult with her and see if she can sense anything amiss in the threads of fate. We need to know for certain who is after Ella so that we can better protect her. You will fortify your concealment illusion." He looks to Cash, Finn, and Devon. "You will check the borders of the spell for any weakness or indication that someone is at the edge of the barrier."

Ella looks to me. "I will go with you so we can begin my training."

Kai's head snaps to her. "You should remain here, in the cottage, where it is safe for now."

"No," she states firmly. "I need to learn how to defend myself. Nyx," she gestures to me, "already agreed to train me."

Kai's blue eyes widen as he turns to me.

Before he can speak, I offer. "She wants to learn. I see no reason not to train her."

Reluctantly, he nods, but it is easy to see in his gaze that he feels I've betrayed him. After all, he is our leader and I should have cleared this with him first.

Ella turns to him. "What do you think happened to the prince? Do you think he's still alive?"

Kai shakes his head. "I do not know."

She reaches out and takes his hand.

His expression softens as he looks to her.

I am irrationally jealous as her blue eyes stare deep into his with a look of concern. "Will it be safe for you to go to the Elder?"

"Yes. I trust her. I have known her since I was a child."

"Please be careful," she says. "I don't want anything to happen to you." Her eyes drift over each of us. "Or any of you."

Kai's gaze darts briefly to mine and I recognize the hope that flashes behind his eyes. Perhaps she is not still angry with him. Only time will tell, I suppose.

As soon as Kai leaves, each of us goes off to tend to our

duties. I promise to return to her as soon as I'm done, so we may begin her training.

I am standing at the edge of the magical barrier, arms raised as I weave more spells into the illusion, when I hear something behind me.

I flick one ear back toward the sound and flare my nostrils. I recognize immediately that it is Ella, but what is she doing here?

When I finish, I turn to face her with a questioning look. "You should be back in the cottage, where it is safe. I promised I would come back as soon as I was finished."

"It's been hours," she says. "I was worried about you."

Her concern touches me deeply. "I appreciate your concern, but I am fine, Ella."

She blinks up at me. "I'd like to stay out here with you."

Her luminous blue eyes search mine. She is the most enchanting creature I have ever seen. How could I deny her anything she wants when she looks at me like that? "All right. But please stay close."

We move from one area to another as I weave more intricate spells into the barrier. She is quiet as I work, but I hear her begin to hum softly behind me after a moment. Her voice is beautiful. I've heard her sing before in the gardens of her home, and so as she begins to sing a soft tune to herself, I do not interrupt.

Clouds begin gathering overhead. A loud crack of thunder startles us both, and I move to her side. "We should return to the cottage."

She nods, and together we race back toward the clearing and the cottage in the center. I make certain she moves through the door first. She turns to me, and she appears miserable. Her entire body shaking, wet and cold.

I take her hand and guide her up the stairs to the bathroom. "You must get out of these clothes and get warm," I tell her.

She nods, and I begin to draw her a warm bath. I make sure to keep my eyes averted from her nude form. As soon as she enters the tub, I go back into the bedroom and stoke the fire to make certain it remains burning to heat the room.

"Nyx?" she calls out, and I rush back to the bathroom.

"Yes?"

"Can you hand me the soap?"

I find the soap and give it to her, making sure not to look upon her as she bathes. I recall how Devon reminded me that humans are embarrassed by their nudity, and I do not wish to make her nervous.

When she is finished bathing, I leave the room so she may change, making sure to leave her a gown and soft robe.

As soon as she enters the bedroom, my jaw drops as my gaze travels over her body. She is more beautiful than any female I have ever seen. The strap of her sleep gown hangs off to one side, baring her shoulder.

The v of the gown dips between the valley of her breast, accentuating the softly rounded globes. Her nipples are easily outlined through the fabric. The two beaded tips straining against the silken material as if begging for my attention.

I am seated on the couch, and I'm surprised as she moves to my side and sits down. So close, her thigh is touching mine. I draw in a shaky breath as she curls one leg beneath her and leans against me.

My nostrils flare as I draw her delicate scent deep into my lungs. My mouth begins to water at the thought of tracing my tongue over her body and through her folds to taste her sweet nectar.

But she does not want me in this way; I do not think.

She sighs in contentment as she nestles into my side.

I wrap one arm around her, pulling her close. "Thank you, Nyx."

"For what?"

"For taking such good care of me. I just want you to know that I appreciate all that you are doing to keep me safe."

I turn to her. "We are your guards. We will always protect you, Ella."

She smiles up at me, and it's the most beautiful thing I have ever seen.

"Tell me about you, Nyx."

I arch a brow. "What would you like to know?"

"Why do you and Devon seem to always be at odds with one another?"

A smile quirks my lips. It seems Ella is rather direct. I like that she gets right to the core of things. "We bicker, yes," I explain, "but we do not hate each other."

"But why do you play tricks on him, like you did with the fountain?"

He laughs softly. "I suppose it is our nature to be slightly adversarial with each other. Rabbit and Cat shifters do not normally mix."

"Why is that?"

"Cats seem to be ... easily annoyed and often quick-tempered," I explain. "Whereas my kind, we... in rabbit shifter litters there are often many children born. So we are very social creatures and often play tricks with each other. Especially our siblings. It is a... type of affection among us, I suppose."

Her brow furrows. "Why are there so many children in rabbit shifter litters?"

A red flush creeps up my neck to my cheeks. I am loath to admit this to her because I fear her rejection. "Rabbits are known for their... stamina."

Her mouth drifts open in shock.

With a heavy sigh, I continue. I do not wish to hold back anything about myself to her. If I want her to choose me, I have to be completely honest in who and what I am. "Our urge to mate is powerful compared to the other shifters," I add. "I am uncertain why it is this way for us. It just is." I pause. "I suppose it is part of my nature that I long for a large family with many kits."

She gives me a curious look. "What do guards do about families if they do not bond to the person they protect?"

I've dreamed of Ella many times, and almost every dream ends with her in my arms as we make passionate love. I desire her to be my mate and to have a family with her.

I swallow thickly. I'm worried that her question may be hinting that she does not desire me and never will as she does Finn and Cash. "Most guards dedicate their entire lives to the one they protect." I cup her chin and meet her gaze evenly. "I have already decided this is what I will do. I want only to guard you and be at your side, Ella. And I understand if you never take me as yours the way you have taken Cash and Finn. After all, as I said, many females do not want to mate a rabbit shifter."

"It's all right," she whispers. "It's just part of who you are. It's nothing to be ashamed of."

I lift my gaze to her. "Many shifter females refuse to mate a rabbit shifter because of it. They refuse cat shifters as well, but for a... different reason," I mumble.

"Well, you don't ever need to be ashamed of who or what you are, Nyx. I will never judge you for it."

"Thank you, Ella."

She gives me a curious look. "Is that why you did not want to look at me while I was bathing? While I was dressing?"

With a slight clench of my jaw, I nod. "You are very beautiful, Ella. I know humans are averse to being observed while they are nude. And also... it stirs something in me to see you. Desires that I... do not believe you will want."

She touches my jaw. "Why would you think I would not want you?"

"Although I have never experienced it, I have heard of the mating frenzy that my people experience. The desire to mate repeatedly is so great… it can be overwhelming for those outside of other rabbit shifters."

Her blue eyes search mine. "Why does this worry you so much?"

I clench my jaw. "I want to be tender and gentle with you. I worry my desires and my needs would be too much. That you would—"

She presses her finger to my lips to silence me. "I am not made of glass. If this is part of who you are, I accept it."

Hope flares inside me. "You do?"

She smiles. "I... I'm not ready to mate, if that's what you are asking. But I... I do feel drawn to you, Nyx. You and the others."

I lower my gaze. "It's the bond, Ella. It makes you feel—"

She presses a finger to my lips to silence me as she softly shakes her head. "It's more than that. I feel it here." She places her hand over her heart.

I frown. "How do you know?"

"Because when I was kissing who I thought was the prince, it felt wrong. It felt wrong the moment his hand touched mine."

With a heavy sigh, I nod. "That is probably because he was not the prince."

"No," she states firmly. "It's because he wasn't you. He wasn't any of my guards. You are the ones I want. The ones I feel drawn to. It felt wrong to give myself to someone else." Her gaze holds mine. "And even if we find the prince alive somewhere, I've already decided."

My brow furrows. "Decided what?"

"That I am not going to be his wife. I will find another way to make him an ally with your people."

My mouth drifts open in shock. We've messed all of this up. Horribly. The Elders and everyone else placed their faith in us. Fate chose us to guide her, and now... we are causing her to divert her path from what the prophecy foretold.

As if sensing my concern, she cups my cheek, guiding my face to hers. "I don't care what the prophecy says. This is my life, and I'm not going to allow anyone to make my decisions for me. Not the Elders, not some ancient scroll and certainly not the prince—if he's still alive somewhere."

She is brave and much stronger than I first realized. Her fragile form belies a strength of will as mighty as any warrior. And I find myself falling for her even more as her determined gaze meets mine, full of conviction. "You are my guard, Nyx, and I want to seal you to me. Do you agree?"

"Yes," I reply without hesitation. I want to be her guard, her lover, her mate, the father of her children. I want all of this and more. But right now, she is simply asking me to bind myself to her as her guard, and this, I will do eagerly. "I can think of no other female I would ever want to dedicate my life to, Ella," I murmur as she moves closer to me.

Her warm breath whispers across my skin as she leans in. "I want to be yours," I breathe as she seals me to her with a vow and her kiss.

Her lips are warm and softer than I imagined, and as her tongue curls around mine, my entire body fills with desire and longing so great it takes everything within me to hold back.

I want to wrap my hands around her waist and flip her onto her stomach, driving into her over and over, filling her with my seed. I curl my hands into fists in my lap, struggling against my urgent need. I want her so much it is painful.

My cock is fully erect and throbbing with the desire to sheathe myself deep inside her warm, wet heat. As she continues to stroke her tongue against mine, I am lost.

She pulls herself into my lap, straddling my hips with her thighs. I gasp as the heat of her center presses against my cock. A sharp hiss escapes me as I struggle to keep from coming right then and there.

"Ella, please," my voice sounds strangled, even to my own ears. "We must stop, or else I fear I may be unable to keep myself from—"

She pulls back, and I already miss the feel of her body pressed against mine. She stares deep into my eyes and nestles against me.

I run my hands through her long silken hair, trying to force my body to calm. I want her so badly; it is torture. But I also do not want to pressure her into mating.

"I'm sorry we did not come to you sooner, Ella," I whisper. My hands trace over her silken gown. The rough lines of the scars on her back are easily felt through the fabric. I clench my jaw. I wish I'd killed the woman who did this to her. "If we'd known what you were going through, we would have come for you sooner."

She shakes her head softly. "It's all right. You're here now," she whispers. "That's all that matters."

My beautiful and brave Ella. I pray she chooses me as hers someday, for I will never want another female but her as my mate.

CHAPTER 24

NYX

It has been two days. Kai has still not returned, and Cash, Finn, and Devon are patrolling the area, searching for any hint of intruders. Devon and I have been relegated to sleeping downstairs the past two nights while Cash and Finn make love to Ella, and not very quietly either, much to our dismay.

Devon acts indifferent, but I'm confident he feels as I do. It is difficult to hear her call out their names when she reaches her peak, knowing that they are allowed to worship her body and give her pleasure while we... are not.

I am happy for my brothers, even if I do envy them.

As I step outside the cottage to fortify the magic barrier, Ella's voice stops me abruptly. "Wait!"

I spin to face her.

She smiles. "Can I come with you?"

"If you wish."

"After you're finished, we can train some more," she offers.

I've been showing her mostly defensive moves the past few days. It is best to start with these first so that if she has need to defend herself, she has the tools to do so. Later on, we will begin moving to more complicated styles of fighting. But for now, she wishes to be able to fend off attackers if she must.

In truth, I love spending time with her and am thrilled she wishes to come with me while I check the barrier.

We are near the property's outer edge, and I'm surprised she has not complained about the long walk. It is quite far, but she seems to enjoy it. And as we continue, we talk back and forth.

When we reach the barrier, I begin a more potent spell. That is why I wished to come out this far. I could have cast a weaker one closer to the cottage, but my nightmares of Ella's death have plagued me the past few nights, and I want to make certain our shields are strong.

As I am casting, Ella begins singing softly behind me. Her lovely voice fills the air, and I am once again completely enchanted by her. When I finish, I creep back to where she is waiting nearby and listen as she sings.

A loud crack of thunder sounds overhead, and dark clouds roll across the sky so quickly, I stare up at them in shock. Is this some kind of side effect of my spell? It is well-known that all magic has consequences, both good and bad. And the power of my spell may be the reason this storm developed so quickly. There is no way it is a naturally occurring event.

The sky seems to open up, and rain pours down in thick sheets. I look at Ella. "We are far from the cottage, but there is a cave nearby. We can shelter there while we wait out the storm."

She nods, her eyes wide. I take her hand, pulling her along behind me as we make our way to the cavern.

Desire burns through my veins so intense I feel as if I can hardly contain it. This, I know for sure, is an effect of the spell casting. It makes everything heightened, including longing and want. Something deep and primal unfurls from inside me at the thought of taking her to the cave. It is as if we are a mated pair and I am taking her to our burrow.

The sounds of her soft cries and moans of pleasure last night made me jealous, but it also stoked the flames of my need. I long to bury myself deep in her warmth. To fill her with my essence and claim her as my mate.

When we reach the cave, I turn to find her thoroughly drenched. Her simple white dress clings tightly to her form, outlining her breasts and the curve of her hips. Cool air blows through the cavern, and her nipples bead from the cold. The perfect outline of them, pink and visible beneath the cloth, makes my mouth water.

I have never seen a more beautiful or tempting creature before. As she moves toward me, I flex my fingers with want to touch her. But I will not unless she asks me to. I do not wish to presume that she wants all of us when she has only chosen Cash and Finn thus far.

I force my gaze away from her and move to find some wood. "I will start a fire to warm us."

She nods and sits on a nearby rock.

Out of the corner of my eye, I notice her shivering slightly. I turn to face her. "You should remove your dress so that we may dry it near the flames."

She gives me a hesitant look as she nervously tucks a stray tendril of hair behind her ear. "Can I ask you something?"

"Of course. Anything."

She carefully removes her wet dress and hands it to me. I spread it out on a rock beside the fire, purposefully making sure to keep my gaze on the ground instead of her body. She is human. Nudity is not as acceptable to her people as it is to mine. And while she has grown more comfortable with me, I dare not presume it is all right to gaze upon her naked form.

"Cash and Finn said it isn't wrong among your... kind to take more than one mate."

My eyes snap up to meet hers, and I notice how she bands one arm across her breasts to hide them from my gaze, as if timid.

She continues, "I know that I've already bound myself to Cash and Finn, but they're twins... and they said they were fine with sharing me, but..." her voice trails off.

I take her hand, anxious to understand what it is that she hesitates to tell me. I hope that she will take all of us as hers, but I don't expect her to do this. I merely pray that it happens. "It is acceptable among our people. Not everyone takes more than one mate, but many of us do. What is wrong, Ella?" I pause as dread settles deep in my stomach. Maybe she is trying to tell me she only wants Cash and Finn. So, I make sure she knows that all of us will understand and honor it if that is her choice. I meet her gaze evenly. "None of us would ever try to pressure you into anything you do not want, Ella. My vow."

"I realize the bond makes me feel closer to you all, but.." She lifts her gaze, her blue eyes staring deep into mine. "It feels like so much more than that."

I tip my head to the side. "How so?"

A shy smile crests her lips. "I have feelings for each of you. Romantic ones. But I... I do not know if it's wrong. I mean... I know you say your kind often take one mate, but would it create problems within the group if I chose to be with all of you?"

My heart begins hammering in my chest as hope flares inside me. "It is not wrong," I quickly reassure her. "We feel the same for you as well."

She blinks up at me. "You do?"

"Yes. But you must choose if you want us. It is the female who decides in our culture."

She moves closer. "And you?" Her voice is full of lust, as her eyes bore deep into mine. "Do you want me, Nyx?"

I reach out and trace my fingers across the petal-soft skin of her cheeks. Her lips part slightly beneath my gaze. "Even now, I desire you more than anything I have ever wanted before," I admit. "And it is difficult to hide this from you."

She takes my hand and entwines our fingers as she pulls me close. "Then, don't."

The last of my control crumbles beneath her words. I wrap my arm around her back and pull her flush against me. My cock is completely engorged and painfully erect against her abdomen. When she reaches down and gently strokes the tip, I hiss through my teeth. "If you do that, I will be tempted to take you right now."

She wraps her delicate hand around my length, staring at me with a half-lidded gaze.

"You are certain?" I rasp.

She nods once.

Dropping the illusion of my clothing, I gather her in my arms and push her back against the cave wall. I pull her legs up over my hips and notch my tip at her entrance.

Her core is already slick with arousal. Her gaze holds mine, and her lips part on a moan as I enter her channel. I thrust deep, sheathing myself completely inside her.

"So tight," I rasp.

I groan as I stroke long and deep into her warm, wet heat. Her body is so soft and giving; I never imagined making love would ever feel like this. It takes all my strength not to come inside her right now.

But I force myself to hold back, wanting to bring her to climax before finding my own. I release a small burst of

173

precum into her channel, and she gasps at the sensation. I need to soften her womb so that she opens to me, accepting my seed and sealing our bond.

She holds tightly to me, digging her nails into my shoulders as I pump into her.

"Oh, Nyx," she moans against my ear.

I capture her mouth with a claiming kiss, stroking my tongue against hers.

She feels so good. I'm barely holding on to my control as I pick up my pace, thrusting hard and deep. I had wanted our first time to be slow and gentle, but my need is too great. The desire to fill her with my seed is like a burning force deep inside me, and I cannot hold back as I thrust into her.

As she approaches the edge of her desire, the small muscles of her channel flex and quiver around my cock. She releases a keening cry as she clamps tightly around my length. Her release triggers my own, and I grasp her hip, holding her firmly in place as my cock begins to pulse. I roar as my release erupts from my body, filling her womb with my essence.

Her entire form goes limp as she comes down from her climax, but I am far from done. I brush the hair back from her face and stare deep into her eyes before capturing her mouth with a branding kiss. "I must have you again," I breathe against her lips.

She stares at me in wonder. "So soon?"

"Yes." I begin to roll my hips against her once more.

Her head falls back, and she moans my name.

My desire for her is so great, I bear her to the floor and begin thrusting into her. My people are known for their stamina and vigorous mating frenzies. I never understood until this moment just how strong the drive to mate could be.

The need to fill her again with my seed is almost

maddening in its intensity. I gaze down at her. Her long, silken hair fans around her head like a beautiful halo. Her lips part as she stares up at me with a half-lidded gaze.

I feel the beginning of her climax as she tightens around my length. I thrust hard and deep and roar out her name as we come together.

Even as I come down from my pleasure, it isn't enough. It is the nature of my kind to mate over and over again. The other shifters often joke about this, but they do not understand the intense need to drive into one's mate several times in one mating. I can barely think beyond the soft feel of her body around mine. Nothing exists outside of this moment with her.

I am almost ashamed, but not too much so to tell her. "Please, I must take you again. I need you."

Panting heavily, she reaches up to cup my cheek. She pulls my face down to hers and presses a soft kiss to my lips. "I am yours," she whispers into my mouth.

Barely able to hold myself back, I stare down at her. "I do not want to hurt you or be too rough."

She gives me a faint smile. "You aren't hurting me, Nyx. I promise. I want all of you. Everything you would give me."

Her words stoke the flames of my desire. I pull back and quickly flip her onto her stomach. I cover her body with mine and band my arms around her waist to hold her flush against me as I whisper in her ear. "Is this all right?"

She nods.

I use my knees to part her thighs then press my cock against her entrance. She moans, and her eyelids flutter open and closed as I enter her from behind.

I pull her back against me as I stroke into her. As I find a rhythm, I begin to move faster, pulling her against me as I drive hard and deep in a furious pace, wanting to push her pleasure to new heights.

She moans my name along with an incoherent string of words as I thrust into her over and over again. When she tightens around me and cries out my name, that is my undoing. I slam my hips against hers and hold her in place as my seed erupts from my body. I hold her tightly to me as I empty myself deep inside her.

As she lies beneath me, panting heavily and spent, my need is still not completely sated. Perhaps it is the knowledge that the prince still lives; therefore, there is always a chance she may choose him over us eventually.

Something dark and primal within me wants to fill her so full of my essence and give her such intense pleasure that she cannot even think of any other male, much less take another as her mate. It will be difficult to share her with my brothers, but not as hard as it would be if she took a human. They do not share, and I would not want to share her with a human male.

Something in the back of my mind prickles my awareness, drawing me out of my lust-filled haze. I look down in shock to find her staring up at me. She reaches up and traces her delicate fingers across my cheek. "I could hear your thoughts, my love. I don't want the prince, Nyx," she whispers. "I never did."

My heart soars, and I smile down at her. I crush my lips to hers and begin to pump inside her again.

Her eyes go wide, and she opens her mouth as if to speak, but then I lift her leg, changing the angle of my thrusts and sinking impossibly deeper. She moans loudly before panting my name.

After taking her at least six times, my need is finally sated. Her body is limp in my arms as she stares up at me, threading her fingers through the hairs at the nape of my neck.

I love her so much; I want everything with her. I reach down and cup her cheek, running my thumb softly along her lower lip. "I have dreamed of making love to you many times, my beautiful Ella. I long to fill you with my essence and have kits with you someday, my beautiful mate."

A slow grin curves her lips. "If we keep making love as many times as we did, it will probably happen sooner than you think."

My brow furrows in confusion. "You would allow yourself to conceive so early in our relationship?"

"Allow myself?" she asks. "It would just happen on its own if we're not careful. Which"—her gaze drops down to our hips, our bodies still joined together—"we're not being careful at all right now. But I love you," she whispers. "All of you, and I'm not worried. If it happens, it happens."

I cup her cheek, searching her eyes. "Human females do not determine when their wombs open up to receive a male's seed? They have no control of the release of their eggs?"

She shakes her head softly. "No. It all depends upon our cycle. If we make love while we're at our fertile peak, conception can happen during that time if we don't take precautions."

Fierce possessiveness fills me as I stare down at her. A low growl of arousal rumbles through me as I slowly begin to roll my hips against hers once more. "And where are you at now in this human cycle of yours?"

"I—" She moans as I stroke long and deep.

I cup her chin, forcing her gaze to mine as I await her answer.

She stares up at me, her eyelids heavy with desire. "If I'm not right at my fertile peak, I am close. It's been a few weeks since my cycle began and—"

I cut her words off with a passionate kiss. Cash and Finn may have mated her first, but I will mate her many more times than they did. I will bring her to climax so that her body will eagerly take in my seed, increasing the chances of it taking root deep in her womb.

It is tradition that a female bear a child to each of her mates if she has more than one. But the intensely possessive part of me wants to be the first to give her a child. I crush my lips to hers as I stroke long and deep inside her core.

A noise outside draws my attention, and I still. "What is —" Ella starts to ask, but I put a finger to her lips to silence her as I train my ears toward the entrance of the cave.

"Who is there?" a deep voice calls out. "Show yourself."

Carefully, I pull away from Ella's body. I motion for her to remain quiet and to hide.

She moves behind a large boulder, and I start toward the entrance to the cave.

I recognize the wolf shifter immediately. I straighten my shoulders and give him an icy glare.

His nostrils flare and he chuckles. "It seems like I interrupted something here."

"This is our cave," I growl. "Go find one of your own."

"And what if I want to join in?" He grins, displaying two sharp rows of teeth.

"I do not share my mate with anyone."

"Is that right?" He arches a brow. "Even if she is human?"

I still.

His grin widens. "I've played with a few of them myself, and I recognize the scent. Let me share in your play, and I promise not to tell anyone."

I growl.

"It is against our laws to mate a human, is it not?" he asks, his eyes narrowing slightly. "And it is also illegal to have her on this side of the veil. Share her with me, and I'll speak of this to no one."

Concentrating, I call upon my magic to conjure my knife —my most deadly possession. The moment I feel the cool steel of the handle in my palm, I rush toward him and pin him back against the wall, holding the blade to his throat.

His eyes are wide in panic and alarm. His kind always underestimates mine, believing us weak because we are rabbit shifters instead of wolves.

"How did you find us here?" I grit through my teeth.

"The rain," he sputters. "It weakened some sort of barrier. A magic one. I wanted to see what it was concealing, and I found you." His eyes dart behind me as if searching for Ella. "But I suppose you are the one who raised it in the first place, aren't you? To conceal your human from our kin."

His words unnerve me. This should not have happened; rain should not affect my magic, unless... I shake my head softly, pushing the thought aside as I question the wolf.

"Why were you here in the first place?"

"The queen," he gasps as I press the blade firmly against his skin, drawing a small trickle of blood. "Her cousin was killed by a human. She suspects that human is here some-where and ordered us to search for her."

My eyes widen slightly at his admission. "What do you know of the queen's cousin?" I ask.

"Only that he was doing her bidding. He disguised himself as the prince and was sent to the human kingdom to kill the Chosen One. The prophecy of the elders," he wheezes against my firm grip. "It's wrong. If we form a treaty with the humans, they will only use it to attack us later. It is not possible to maintain peace with their kind. She has ordered everyone to seek out the Chosen One. We must kill her before she fulfills the prophecy and dooms our people."

"What else do you know?"

"Nothing," he begs. "I swear."

I focus on his eyes and recite the spell of truth. He stares at me but says nothing, and I know that he was not lying. If he were, the magic would have compelled him to speak further. I cannot allow him to live, however. And after his threat toward my mate, I would not want to anyway.

In one swift movement, I drag the knife across his throat.

A sharp inhalation behind me draws my attention, and I spin to find Ella staring at his bloodied form with wide eyes.

"They want to kill me," she whispers, her eyes staring down at him in shock. "They're searching for me, Nyx."

I rush forward and take her in my arms. "We will not let them."

When we return to the cottage, everyone is already waiting.

Kai gives me a furious look. His nostrils flare and he narrows his eyes. "Where were you? We were worried."

It is easy to tell that he knows I have mated Ella. I know I should not have kept her away for so long, but it was challenging to sate my mating lust once it had begun. He would not understand. His kind does not experience this like mine does.

"A wolf shifter found us," I tell him. "I killed him, but not before he informed me that it was the queen's cousin that Ella killed at the castle. The wolves are searching for Ella. Our queen has ordered every shifter to hunt her down and kill her before she can fulfill the prophecy."

Kai's expression does not waver, telling me that this is not news to him.

He clenches his jaw. "I spoke with the Elder. She said as much to me also. It seems the queen does not want to give up her power."

"What do you mean?" Ella asks.

"You are destined not only to unite our two kingdoms but to become the queen of our kingdom as well, thus overthrowing the reign of our current queen and her wolf pack."

"What are we going to do?"

"Nothing for now," Kai replies. "We will hide here while we decide upon our next move." His gaze shifts to me. "Reestablish the protective barrier," he orders.

"I will."

Kai's blue eyes meet mine. "How was it weakened in the first place?"

I look at Ella. "The wolf claimed it was the rain, but rain should not affect my magic, unless it was enchanted."

Devon frowns. "Enchanted?"

"Yes." I look at Ella. "When you sang, it brought the rain with it. It happened yesterday and in the gardens of your home as well. I did not recognize the magic of it then, but I do now. You are the reason your land has prospered while all else has withered and dried up. You have the ability to summon the rain."

Cash turns to her. "I've heard her father's line had this ability—mastery over one of the elements."

"Yes," Finn adds. "But it was always believed to be a myth."

CHAPTER 25

ELLA

"How is this possible? Why does my singing cause it to rain?"

Finn looks to me. "It is said that it was a gift to your father's line from one of our earliest queens. A token of friendship and prosperity between our two people. She gifted the magic of the elements to each of the four human kingdoms that were allied with our people."

Kai looks to me, his expression sober. "There is more."

"What is it?"

"Someone casts a spell on the body of the wolf shifter that you killed to make sure he remained in the prince's form." He pauses. "The entire kingdom is searching for you. They believe that you lured and then murdered their prince."

"Who would do this?"

"Our wolf shifter queen."

"But why?" I shake my head in confusion. "I've never done anything to her, let alone know who she is. Before all this, I didn't even know that shifters existed."

"According to the Elder, you are not just chosen to unite the two kingdoms. You are destined to become the queen of all shifters."

I shake my head. "Why me?"

"Because your ability to understand our mind speech is the bridge that can unite our two kingdoms. But your power to heal the land—in the form of conjuring rain—can bring prosperity to both shifters and humans as well."

"Does the Elder know what happened to the true prince?"

"Our queen has him under her spell and locked away somewhere in hiding."

"Why not just kill him and be done with it?" I ask. "Why did she keep him alive?"

"I do not know," Kai replies. "But I have a theory."

"What is it?"

"I believe she wants to use him as a pawn to take power. But first, she must ensure you are dead. His people search for you because his parents believe that you killed him. Once you are dead, she will produce the real prince and ask for the throne in return for giving him back to his family."

My mouth drifts open in shock.

Kai continues. "She wants you dead so that none may challenge her right to rule."

"And what about the prince?" I ask, trying to find a loophole in this prophecy. "The prophecy says I'm supposed to marry him. Does the Elder still believe this too?"

Kai lowers his head, nodding grimly.

I curl my hands into fists at my side as I struggle to push down my anger and frustration. "I won't do it," I grind out. "No one is going to force me to do it either."

Kai's eyes snap up to meet mine. "That is what the Elders sent us to you for. We are supposed to see the prophecy fulfilled. We must rescue the prince and—"

I cut him off abruptly as I glare at him. "I don't care what the prophecy says. It's my decision, and I won't let you deliver me into someone else's hands. Especially after what happened the first time."

"We did not know that it was not the prince, Ella. I am sorry," he says, his gaze filled with regret. "If we had known—"

"I don't care if it's the prince or not. I won't marry someone only to fulfill a prophecy. I trusted you, Kai, and I nearly paid for it with my life."

He visibly flinches at my words as if struck.

Nyx steps forward. "It was not just Kai," he says. "We all share the blame, Ella."

Tears sting my eyes, but I blink them back.

Kai opens his mouth to speak, but I turn away. "I don't care what you say. I won't do it. I won't marry the prince if he's still alive. I don't care what the prophecy says. I won't be used ever again."

I run up the stairs to the bedroom, leaving him and everyone else down below. How could he even think to ask me to marry the prince after everything that has happened? After I've already mated Cash, Finn, and Nyx? No. I shake my head firmly. I won't give them up just to fulfill some stupid prophecy.

When my father died, I lost everyone I ever loved. And now that I have Cash, Finn, and Nyx, I refuse to lose anyone else.

CHAPTER 26

KAI

"Y ou are a fool," Nyx shakes his head at me. "How could you think to ask her to consider marrying the prince? Especially after what happened?"

"I—"

"Besides"—Cash steps forward, and levels a dark gaze at me—"She has already chosen us. Or do you not remember this?"

Finn's eyes burn with anger. "I will not give up Ella. Not now. Not ever."

"Neither will I," I swear. "I do not care about the prophecy." I give them a pleading look. "You think I want to lose her as well?"

"You never had her," Nyx snaps. "Not like we do." He looks to Cash and Finn to send the message, and the message is clear. They have bonded to Ella; she has taken them as her mates. We may be bond brothers, but now they have crossed the line into being bonded mates, something Devon and I are not a part of.

Jealousy burns through me like fire. "It is true. She has not chosen me. But that does not mean I want her to choose the prince." I look down at my hands. "The Elder said that if she did not marry the prince, she could die."

Devon blinks at me in shock. "What? How?"

"I... do not know. She said she could not see beyond Ella's decision to take the prince as her mate or not. And so, she believes it means Ella will die is she does not marry him."

Nyx clenches his jaw. "Even so. It should be Ella's decision. We cannot force her or push her to do something she does not wish."

I run my hand roughly through my hair. "I only want for her safety, above all else. If not for the risk of her dying, I never would have even suggested she still marry the prince. I no longer care about the prophecy. All I care about is her."

Nyx puts a hand on my shoulder and meets my eyes evenly. "Then, tell her this. Because right now, she believes you want to give her up because you care more for the prophecy than for her feelings."

I grit my teeth in frustration. He is right. I lift my gaze to the staircase. I have to find a way to fix this between us. I cannot bear for her to hate me.

CHAPTER 27

KAI

As soon as I enter the bedroom, I find her lying on the bed, her shoulders shaking as she sobs into her pillow.

I move to her side and place my hand over hers. "Ella?" I whisper, but she pulls her hand away as if burned by my touch. "Please," I plead. "Let me explain."

She lifts her tear-stained face to meet mine. "Explain what? How you want to pawn me off to another male? How you want to give me to someone I don't love like you did the first time? You don't care about me. If you did, you would never ask me to marry someone else." She lowers her head and cries into the pillow. "I hate this bond. It makes me feel close to you. Makes me trust you. And I—" her voice breaks. "I love you, but you don't love me. You can't, or else you'd never ask me to marry the prince, prophecy or not."

I pull her into my arms. She struggles weakly in my hold before burying further into my chest as she sobs against me.

"I hate you. I hate that I love you, and you don't love me. I hate you, Kai."

I hold her tightly to me, smoothing my hand over her back and shoulders as I speak softly. "You are wrong, Ella. I love you. More than anything."

She lifts a tear-filled gaze to me. "Then why do you still want me to marry the prince?"

"Because I'm scared," I admit.

"I... I don't understand." She sniffs. "You aren't making any sense."

I tell her what the Elder conveyed about the probability of death in her vision. I press a tender kiss to her forehead and cup her cheek as I stare deep into her blue eyes. "I cannot stand the thought of you dying. Even if it means giving you up, I would do it... just so that you may live."

She shakes her head. "But you don't know that she's right. It may be that she just cannot see my future clearly."

"But Nyx's dreams confirm her visions."

She frowns. "What do you mean?"

As if my very thoughts have summoned him, Nyx appears at the top of the stairs. "It's true, Ella. I have had a recurring nightmare of the Wolf Queen coming for you. In my dreams, she—" he stops, unable to speak it aloud.

"She kills me," Ella finishes his sentence. "You told me this. But maybe your dream is a warning, and it will help us to avoid any danger."

Nyx shakes his head. "We may have already failed. Our recent actions may have only endangered you further."

Her small brow furrows deeply. "What do you mean?"

I meet her gaze evenly. "I fear that Nyx's dreams may have foretold what has happened now. In taking Cash, Finn, and Nyx as your mates, you do not want the prince. The Elder said they saw your death if you did not marry him.

And if you refuse to give them up so that you can marry the prince and fulfill the prophecy, you might die.

Indignation burns in her eyes. "I don't care. I won't marry the prince. I refuse to be handed off to another as if my choice doesn't matter." She looks to Nyx, tears filling her eyes. "And you? How could you even think to ask me to marry the prince? Especially after what we just—" Her voice catches as tears spill down her cheeks.

Nyx rushes toward her, gathering her in his arms as he pulls her close to his chest. "I cannot bear the thought of you dying. Not for me, Ella. Not if loving me means that you will die. I do not want to give you up, but I will not force you to be mine if you want to be released from our bond to save your life."

She touches his face. "I don't want to lose you, Nyx. Not now. Not ever. You are my mate, and I will not give you up."

I gently touch her cheek, drawing her attention to me. "Please understand. I only wanted you to marry the prince to keep you from dying, Ella. That is the only reason I would ever even suggest it."

She pulls away from my touch as if burned. "I would rather risk death than marry someone I don't love."

I clench my jaw as I give her a solemn nod. "I understand this now. Forgive me. I should have realized it should be your decision. I am sorry, Ella. I have heard that if you love someone, you only want what is best for them." I stare deep into her eyes. "I love you, Ella. With everything that I am. And I am so afraid to lose you. If anything were to happen, I do not think I could bear it. I would—"

Cash and Finn come into the room and move to her side. With a slight clench of my jaw, I meet her eyes evenly. "I'm sorry, Ella."

I look again at Nyx, Cash, and Finn. They are already

bonded to her. Of course, I am happy for them, but I can hardly bear the deep ache in my chest as I watch them touch her so tenderly, knowing she has already chosen them. I turn to leave. "I will check the perimeter," I speak over my shoulder.

I quickly shift and fly out the window before she or anyone else can respond.

As I fly through the forest, her words replay in my mind. "I hate you," she cried against my chest.

My heart breaks into a million pieces, hearing the words echo through my mind over and over. I love her. With all that I am. But she believes I do not love her... and she hates me for it.

CHAPTER 28

KAI

The next few days pass quickly as I busy myself flying the perimeter to make certain no one else finds us here. I can hardly bear to be in Ella's presence for long, knowing how strongly she feels about me.

I hate you. The words repeat in my mind as pain stabs at my chest.

When I return to the cottage, I find her alone upstairs. Anger fills me that she has been left here by herself. I growl low in my throat. "Where is everyone else? Why did they leave you here?"

She steps toward me and takes my hand. "They left because I asked them to. I wanted to talk to you. Spend time with you. Alone," she adds.

My anger instantly dissipates. "What did you wish to speak of?"

She reaches up to touch my cheek, and I go still, waiting to see what she will do. "You said you loved me."

I place my hand over hers. "More than anything, Ella."

"Then, why did you leave? Why have you been avoiding me these past few days?"

I turn my face into her palm and close my eyes briefly against the pain. Sadness fills me so great I feel as if I am drowning in it. "You said you hate me. And I—" my voice catches. "I cannot bear it."

She places two fingers up under my chin, tipping my head up to hers. "I don't hate you, Kai. I was angry. I'm sorry."

I barely manage to nod as painful memories rush through me. "It is all right. I am used to rejection."

"What do you mean?"

I hesitate, uncertain if I wish to share my past with her.

"Kai," she whispers. "Please, tell me what you mean."

With a slight clench of my jaw, I draw in a deep and steeling breath before I begin. "I was rejected by my family after I left. All of us were taken for training when we were children because we had the mark." I look down at the mark on my left forearm.

"Why did they reject you?" she asks, her gaze pinning mine full of sadness. "Why would they do that?"

"Because bird shifters are a tightly knit family. Our bonds are some of the strongest among our kind. When the Elders removed me from my parents and my siblings... they had to sever the bond to my family. They did this to bond me to my brothers."

"Sever it? What do you mean?"

"They used magic to break my familial bond with my parents and siblings. If they had not, I would have been unable to bond with my brothers."

She gasps as tears fill her eyes. "Oh, Kai, I'm so sorry. You gave up so much to be my guard, and I—I'm not worth it."

I grip her chin firmly, tipping her face back up to mine. "Yes, you are. You are worth every sacrifice I have ever made, and if I had to choose to do it all over again, I would. Now that I know you, I cannot imagine dedicating my life to anyone else, Ella. You are brave, smart, and beautiful. And if you think I do not love you, you are wrong." I pause. "I love you so much that I would let you go... marry the prince even if it would kill me inside, because it would mean that you would live, my beautiful Ella."

She shakes her head softly. "But don't you understand? I don't want the prince. I want you. All of you. And it's not just the bond making me feel like this."

I blink at her as hope flares inside me.

She continues. "When you found me, after I'd killed the wolf shifter, I was so glad to see you, Kai. I swore to myself then that because I had lived and been given a second chance, that I would give myself to you. I love you." She takes my hand and places my open palm directly over her heart. "In my heart, I knew when I first met all of you that you were mine. And not just as my guards. I knew you were supposed to be my mates."

She cups her hand to the back of my neck pulling my face down until it hovers just above hers. "You say that you love me," she whispers. Her luminous ocean-blue eyes search mine. "Show me, Kai," she breathes against my lips. "Show me how much you love me."

I lift her into my arms and move us to the bed, gently laying her atop the covers. I place my arms on either side of her body as I move over her. Her gaze holds mine before I dip my head to the curve of her neck and shoulder. I trace my tongue over the hollow at the base of her throat, feeling the fluttering pulse beneath her petal-soft skin.

Her delicate fragrance surrounds me as I kiss a heated trail down her neck to the v of her chest. I grasp the neckline of her dress and pull it down, revealing the soft, creamy mounds of her breasts. The soft, pink nipples tighten in hard-beaded tips beneath my gaze. I close my mouth over her left breast, laving my tongue across the stiff peak.

A low moan escapes her as she arches up into me. She gasps as I take the hard tip lightly between my teeth. My nostrils flare as the scent of her arousal blooms around us.

"You still carry Nyx's scent," I whisper as I flick my tongue across the sensitive bead of flesh.

She inhales sharply, threading her fingers through my hair as she pulls me against her as if asking for more.

"I will fill you so full of my essence it will erase the scent of him entirely," I growl.

She lifts her head to look down at me in confusion. "But I thought it was acceptable to take more than one mate according to your culture?"

"It is." I press a tender kiss to her soft lips. "But that does not mean I won't be jealous every now and then." I gently nip at her neck and flick my tongue out to taste the sweet salt of her skin. "I *will* want you all for myself from time to time."

I dip my hand beneath the hem of her dress, skimming the tips of my fingers up her thigh, seeking the warm, wet heat of her center. As soon as I reach her folds, I love that she is already slick with arousal. "I want you, Ella," I breathe low in her ear, before trailing a line of kisses down the elegant curve of her neck. "Do you want me?"

CHAPTER 29

ELLA

"Yes," I reply in a breathless whisper. "I want you, Kai."

He takes my breast in his mouth again, catching the hard nub between his teeth. A soft moan escapes my lips as he flicks his tongue over the sensitive peak.

I inhale sharply as his fingers move through my slick folds, and he finds the small bundle of nerves at the cleft.

Encouraged by my response, he continues to brush his thumb over the same spot, driving me mad with desire. I run my fingers through his golden hair, enjoying the silken feel of it as his tongue continues to tease at my breast. He begins a gentle suction that sends ripples of pleasure straight down to my core. Heat pools deep inside me. I want him so much.

My body aches with want for him to fill me, and when I cannot take it anymore, I reach for his cock. He's so thick my fingers cannot quite reach all the way around him, and when I lightly stroke his length, he groans low in his throat.

"Ella," he breathes. "Are you trying to kill me, my beloved?"

Before I can answer, he kisses me long and deep. His tongue strokes against mine in a claiming kiss, stealing the breath from my lungs.

When he pulls away, I let out a small whimper of disappointment. But I only have a moment to feel this way as he sits back on his knees and grips my thighs, pulling me toward him.

He drags my hips up his legs. Liquid beads on the tip of his cock as he draws me closer, notching his crown at my entrance. His mouth falls open as he stares down at where our bodies will join. "You are so beautiful, Ella," he breathes as he slowly pushes into me, inch by agonizing inch.

My head falls back at the delicious feeling of being completely filled by him. He leans forward before stroking long and deep as he stares into my eyes. His gaze is fiery and possessive as he grips my hips, anchoring me to him.

I run my hands down his back, feeling his muscles flex with each thrust beneath the tips of my fingers. He kisses me like a man possessed, running his fingers through my hair and swallowing my moans of pleasure as he strokes his tongue against mine.

"Oh, Ella," he breathes. "You're so tight, my love. As if you don't want to let me go."

"I don't," I whisper against his lips. "I want you, Kai. Forever."

He smiles. "I am yours, my Ella. Always."

He wraps his hands under my back lifting me as he sits back on his heels again. I wrap my legs around his back as he reaches up under my arms to cup my shoulders, pulling me down to meet each thrust of his hips up into my body.

He takes my breast into his mouth as I hold tightly to

him. "You're so soft and warm, my love," he whispers against my skin. "I want to taste all of you."

Everything feels so sensitive like this as he thrusts up into me, filling me completely. His mouth on my breast makes everything that much more intense.

Pleasure coils tight in my core as I run my fingers through his hair and down his back, completely awash in sensation. I begin panting his name as desire builds deep inside me. My toes curl as I move closer to the edge, digging my nails into the thick muscles of his back.

"Open for me, Ella," he whispers. "Take everything so that I can seal you to me, my beautiful mate."

I remember that shifter females can decide when to open their womb to receive their mate's seed, and I realize this is what they've each asked of me, not knowing that my body does not work that way. I'm already open to them. When they fill me, I take their essence deep into my womb each time. "I want you, Kai," I whisper against his lips.

His eyes meet mine; his pupils blow wide so that only a thin rim of blue remains along the outer edges. He holds me tightly to him as he pumps his hips up into me. My pleasure builds like a giant wave before pushing me over the edge, crying out his name as wave after wave of pleasure moves through me.

He thrusts hard and deep and holds me tightly to him, his grip on my body almost bruising as his cock begins to pulse. He roars my name and then erupts deep inside me, filling me with intense heat that seems to go on forever, triggering another orgasm deep within me, this one even more intense than the last.

As I come down from my pleasure, he hugs me to him. His cock is still hard and buried inside me. He captures my mouth in a claiming kiss. He brushes the hair back from my face as he stares deep into my eyes. "You are mine, Ella. And I will never let you go."

"Not even to the prince?" I arch a brow.

He growls and kisses me hungrily. He lays me onto my back on the bed as he begins to move deep inside me again. "Never," he breathes between kisses. "You are mine."

Morning light begins to invade the room around us as I snuggle against Kai's chest. My body aches between my thighs, but in a pleasant way. We made love five times last night, and so I'm surprised when I feel his hard length pressing insistently against my stomach.

He wraps his arms around me and rolls onto his back, setting me on top so that my thighs straddle him. He lifts me just enough to put his crown at my entrance and slowly lowers me onto his cock.

My head falls back, and I moan as he fills me. He grips my hips firmly then begins grinding against me. The friction between us so intense, I'm so close to the edge, and we've only just started.

He pulls my lips down to his and smiles against them. "You are perfect, Ella."

As he moves deep inside me, I'm so sensitive from last night it's almost too much. It's as if my body is both trying to take him deeper and yet push him away at the same time. As if sensing this, he holds my hips even tighter and closes his mouth over my breast.

It sends me spiraling over the edge, and I'm crying out his name as intense pleasure washes over and through me.

His cock pulses deep in my channel and an intense burst of heat fills my core as he cries out my name as he finds his release.

I collapse on top of him in a boneless heap. My entire body completely spent and sated. He carefully lifts me into his arms and takes me to the bath. Together, we sink into the tub as he settles my back against his chest.

He combs his fingers through my hair as he bathes me. When his hand drifts down to the juncture between my thighs, my head falls back against his shoulder, and I moan.

"I need you again, Ella," he whispers against my ear.

He carefully lifts me up and onto his fully engorged and erect cock. It doesn't take long for me to climax, and then he's filling me again. However, this time, he stays seated deep inside me as he drains the tub, not leaving my body until the water is completely gone.

When he lifts us out of the tub, he gently towels me off. Some of his essence runs down my inner thighs as I stand. He gathers some of it with his fingers rubbing it over my skin, and I realize he is covering me with his scent.

I look up at him, wondering at this.

He kisses me long and deep. "I love that you carry the combined scent of our mating. I want everyone to know you are mine."

I wrap my arms around his neck. It seems that my Kai is possessive. I smile against his lips as he kisses me again. I love this about him. It feels good to be treasured and cherished.

After we get dressed, we go down the stairs to find Nyx, Cash, and Finn making breakfast.

I walk over to Cash and Finn, each of them dusted with flour from making biscuits. I reach up and wipe the flour from Cash's nose and press a kiss to his lips. He groans into my mouth as I pull my body against his.

Warm hands wrap around my waist, and I turn to find Finn staring down at me with a hungry gaze. He leans forward and kisses me long and deep. Nyx comes up behind me and pulls me back against him, cupping my breasts in his hands as he kisses my neck.

When I look across the room, I notice Devon's eyes upon us, his gaze full of both longing and rejection. I walk toward him, reaching down to cup his cheek as he stares up at me from the couch. "Why?" he barely manages.

My brow furrows. "'Why what?" I ask, confused.

He lifts his hand to my cheek, tracing his thumb across my lower lip. "You have chosen everyone else. Why not me? Is it because you do not know if you want me? Are you afraid because of what I am?"

He looks so vulnerable right now that my heart breaks for him. I shake my head softly. "Afraid?" I ask, because I don't understand. "Devon, I—"

A harsh knock at the door startles us. Kai moves to answer it.

CHAPTER 30

DEVON

Kai opens the door to find Rina—the peacock shifter—on the other side. He stares at her in disbelief. "Why are you here? How did you even find this place?"

She blinks up at him. "The dress," she explains. "It was created with my magic. All I had to do was follow its threads, and it led me here."

I move from behind him and narrow my eyes, growling at her. "How dare you track us with magic like that," I grit through my teeth. "You have put our female in danger."

"Please." She bows low. "That was not my intent."

"Then why are you here?"

"The king and queen... they've taken my husband. They would have taken me as well, but I escaped. They think we had something to do with their son's assassination since we accompanied Ella to the ball the night that he died and she disappeared."

Worried, I scan the area behind her, half expecting to find

soldiers descending upon this place to take Ella away. After a moment, I turn my attention back to Rina. "The real prince wasn't murdered."

She blinks up at me in shock. "What? How can that be? He lies in state in the castle even now. The queen is beside herself with her grief and will not allow them to bury her son. She keeps him in a glass coffin."

Ella comes up beside me. "He is telling the truth. It wasn't the prince. It was a wolf shifter."

Rina's eyes go wide then fill again with tears. She grips Ella's hand in her own. "Please. You must help me. They are going to hang my husband for this if we do not stop them."

Ella looks at us. "We have to go to the castle. Is there a way to lift the enchantment so the queen can see that it is not her son?"

With a slight clench of my jaw, I nod. I'm reluctant to tell her how to lift the spell because it means she must accompany us there. And the last thing I want is for her to be in danger because I somehow doubt the king and queen will listen to us long enough to allow us to explain. It's more likely they'll immediately place us in the dungeon and execute us all for the prince's murder.

"What do we have to do?" Ella asks.

"Only the one who took his life can lift the spell."

"How?"

"A drop of your blood on his skin will break the enchantment, for it is a blood curse that hides his true form, and only blood can erase it."

Ella gives me a determined look. "All right," she says. "Let's go. We have to save Rina's husband, and we have to find the true prince, wherever he is."

CHAPTER 31

DEVON

As we make our way to the castle, I struggle to quell my fear. Each step toward the palace is one step closer to danger. I glance at my bond brothers beside me and know without asking that they feel the same.

Nyx is skilled in illusory magic. He cast an enchantment on my eyes to make them appear human. Even so, I cannot help but worry that someone might see past it. Drawing in a deep breath, I push down my fear as we continue on.

When we reach the palace gates, each of us appears dressed in only the finest of clothing as we request an audience with the king and queen.

"What business do you have with them?" the guard asks. "They are mourning their son."

I turn to Ella, her hands bound behind her back as if she were my prisoner. She and Rina both. "We have brought the ones responsible for justice."

His eyes snap toward Rina and Ella, and his jaw drops.

"Open the gates!" he cries out. "Tell the king and queen we have found the prince's murderer!"

Guards rush toward the palace. I grip Ella's arm to keep her close to me, but the guard grabs her forearm. "I will take this filth from you."

"No!" I snap, and I feel Kai and Nyx tense beside me as well. "I will take her before the king and queen. There is a reward, is there not?"

He narrows his eyes and gives me a reluctant nod. "Fine," he says. "Follow me."

Leading us to the throne room, the guards watch us warily, their eyes full of anger. One of them steps forward and spits at Ella as he slaps at her face. I rush him, pinning him back against the wall. "Do not touch her," I grind out.

"Why?" he asks angrily. "That witch killed our prince! I was there that night! She bewitched him and murdered him!"

"Take us to the king and queen," Kai snaps. "Now!"

The guard shoves away from me and continues leading us through the palace.

When we reach them, the king is sitting on his throne, while his wife is seated next to the body, laid out in a glass coffin upon a long slab, that she believes is her son. Her face is puffy and swollen from crying, and when she turns to see Ella and Rina, she grits through her teeth. "How could you? How could you kill my son? What did he do to you that would make you do something like this?"

Ella steps forward and bows low. "I did not kill your son."

The queen scoffs.

Ella lifts her head to meet her eyes evenly. "That man is not your son. The body is enchanted. You are shedding tears for a stranger. A wolf shifter."

The king gasps, and so does the queen.

She gives Ella a strange look. "What do you mean?"

"I can prove it," Ella announces, lifting her head proudly.

"She speaks the truth," Kai adds beside me as he bows low to the king and queen. "Allow her to prove it."

Something akin to hope fills the queen's expression as she moves away when Ella steps forward. I hand Ella a knife, and she drags the blade across her palm. Holding it over the body, she allows a few drops of blood to land on his skin.

A rippling wave of light moves over the body then lifts away, disappearing into smoke and taking the false form of the prince with it.

The king and queen stare down at the stranger's form. A broken sob escapes the queen as she turns and hugs the king tightly. "It's not our boy! It isn't our son!"

She turns to Ella. "Where is our son then if this is not him? I don't understand."

As Ella explains everything that happened to them, they listen intently. At the end of their conversation, the king orders his guards to free Rina's husband.

The queen takes Ella's hand. "Please. Is there any way to find our son? You must help us."

Rina steps forward. "There is a way," she says.

"What is it?" the king demands.

"I—" Rina stops, her gaze shifts to me. I do not know what she means to say, but it is easy to see that whatever it is will reveal to them that she is a shifter. Humans used to hunt our kind. What she does is a significant risk to herself and her husband.

I place a hand on her shoulder. "If it goes badly, we will protect you."

She nods and turns back to the king and queen. She allows herself to transform before their eyes into a beautiful peacock, spreading her feathers wide.

The queen stares down at her in shock a moment before she returns to her human form. She bows low, her body trembling as she straightens again. "I am a shifter, Your

Majesties," she explains. "I infuse the clothing I create for my customers with some of my magic, and because of this, I am able to track it. I have made many things for the royal family, and if the prince wore anything I created when taken, I would be able to find him."

The queen takes the king's hand, her grip so tight her knuckles begin to turn white as she stares at Rina. "Please," she begs. "Do whatever you must to find my son."

Rina's husband walks in with the guards. As soon as he sees her, he rushes forward and embraces her.

"Is your husband also a shifter?" the king asks, and Rina's husband pales.

He looks to his wife. "You told them?" he asks, his voice full of alarm. "They will surely kill us now. Their people hunt shifters."

Ella steps forward. "No more," she states firmly, as she meets the eyes of the king and queen. "It is wrong to condemn someone to death simply because they are different."

The king gives her an imperious look as he gestures to the dead body beside them. "And what of this? It was shifters who took my son and replaced him with one of their own, was it not?"

Ella straightens her shoulders as she stands before him, her expression firm. "You cannot judge all people by the actions of only a few."

The king's gaze holds hers, but he says nothing. After a moment, the queen turns to him. "She's right, Victor."

"Shifters are dangerous," he says as he narrows his eyes at Rina and her husband. "Their kind have killed many of ours." He turns his attention to Ella. "Are you a shifter as well?"

She shakes her head. "No, I'm not."

I note she does not reveal that the rest of us are. She is cautious, not trusting the king not to harm us.

"Our people have murdered many shifters as well," Ella adds. "Where does the bloodshed end if not here? Today?"

The king considers her a moment, then stands. "If you find my son, I will consider it."

Ella looks to Rina, then the queen. "We will find your son, and we will return him to you."

CHAPTER 32

ELLA

As we leave the palace, the guards watch us with narrowed eyes. They trust us even less than they did before, now that they know Rina and her husband are shifters.

Kai takes my hand. "You were very brave, my love."

I smile. "So were you."

He lifts my hand to his face, pressing a soft kiss to the space between my thumb and forefinger. Once we are outside the palace gates, he turns to Rina. "What do you need to do to find the prince?"

"I must go back to my shop. The sewing machine is enchanted. It carries the memory of each thread that passes through it. I will call upon the magic within to help me find the prince."

I don't quite understand how it will work, but I only hope that it will. If the prince is wearing something not made by Rina, I don't know how we'll find him.

As if sensing my troubled thoughts, Devon turns to me.

"If Rina cannot locate the prince, we will have to go before the wolf shifter queen. I suspect she will have the answers we seek. It was her cousin who lay dead in the castle; there is no denying she had a hand in this plot." He looks to Kai. "The words of the Elder confirmed it as well."

When we reach Rina's shop, she leads us inside, locking the door behind us. She moves to the back, and I notice the sewing machine in the corner. I blink in astonishment as I watch it working on its own, creating a fine dress before my eyes.

Rina turns to me and smiles. "It is how I get my creations done quickly."

I turn to Nyx, remembering his gift with illusion magic. "Does every shifter have a magical ability of some sort?"

He shakes his head. "Not all practice the arts. It takes great concentration and years of patience to master a particular type of magic."

"What made you want to learn illusion magic?" I ask, curious to know.

"My family is rabbit shifters. As such, we are underestimated by many others. Specifically, the larger shifters," he says. "I have found illusion magic can make us appear much larger or greater in number than we actually are, thus intimidating a foe. It can also shield us from danger by hiding us behind magical barriers, such as the one I placed around the cottage."

This makes sense. I understand now why he would choose to learn these types of spells.

Rina closes her eyes and begins speaking a string of strange words. After a moment, she lifts her gaze to us. "The prince is in a tower on an estate near the edge of the dark forest. It is one of the only green spaces for many miles around it." She cocks her head to the side. "It is odd, is it not? So that should not be too difficult to find."

I look to Kai and the others. "She is describing my home. But why would he be there?"

A loud knock from the front of the store startles me.

Rina looks to us. "I'll go see who it is. I will be back shortly."

She leaves to go to the front of the store.

A scream pierces the air, stopping my heart, followed by a loud crash and growling.

Devon grips my forearm, pulling me behind him as Kai and everyone else moves in front of me as well. I'm so terrified I can barely breathe as we wait while Devon goes to the door. Carefully, he pulls it open and peers into the room.

He bristles and begins growling. "Who are you?" he asks in a low and threatening voice. "Why are you here?"

"I've come to speak with the girl," a man's voice answers, and I note the gravelly rasp of his tone.

"There is no girl," Devon replies. "Leave. Now. Before I end you."

"I can scent her," the man replies. "I know she is here. I mean her no harm. I merely wish to speak with her. It is about the prince."

I push past my mates and step through the door into the front entry room. I notice Rina is unharmed and standing off to one side, her eyes trained on the man. "What about the prince?" I ask, but then still. My entire body begins trembling as the man stares at me, partially shifted in his wolf form.

Sensing my fear, he changes until he appears completely human. He bows low. "Forgive me, my lady. I mean you no harm. My vow. Yes, I am a wolf shifter, but I am not an ally of the queen. She convinced her cousin to take the prince's form because she wanted to stop the prophecy from being fulfilled. She does not want peace because it threatens her rule."

"Why are you here?" I ask, still not sure why he is telling

us all of this. He is a wolf shifter. He could be trying to get us to let down our guard so he can kill us himself.

Kai and the others must be thinking the same because they stand protectively around me in a semicircle, ready to attack at a moment's notice.

"When I was a child, half of our pack was killed by humans. I have lived in fear since that day of losing everyone else because of the hatred between our two peoples." He places his hand on his chest. "Some in the pack want vengeance, but I want peace. I want to live in a world where we do not have to worry about killing one another." He pauses. "I was there the day the queen spoke with one of the Elders. They told her that her reign would soon end and you would be upon her throne instead."

"But I'm human," I tell him. "I don't understand."

He shifts into a wolf, and my mates pull me behind them, growling low in their throat.

He tips his head to the side and speaks in my mind. *"Can you hear me?"*

"Yes," I reply, and he instantly turns into a man once more.

"Then it is true. You are a human who can both hear and speak to our people in our animal form. You are the bridge between worlds." He drops to one knee and bows before me. "You are destined to marry the prince and become the queen of both kingdoms."

Everyone remains still and quiet beside me. The weight of his words hangs heavy in the air. I have already chosen them as my mates. I cannot marry the prince. He is human, and he would not tolerate me having anyone but him. And I do not love him. Nor would I ever love anyone enough to give up my mates.

I do not tell him this, however. I simply motion for him to stand. "Will you help us rescue the prince?"

He crosses his arm over his chest and bows low. "Yes, I will help you." His eyes meet mine. "The prince must kill the wolf queen. It is the only way to transfer the power of the throne. He will not defeat her easily."

I look at my mates. In their eyes, I see the same mistrust that I'm sure my own reflect. I want to believe this man wants to help us, but it could just as easily be a trap set by the wolf queen.

Although I already know the answer, I study him, deciding to test his loyalty. "Do you know where the wolf queen keeps the prince?"

"Yes. He is in a tower near the edge of the forest. You know it well, I presume, for it used to be your home." He pauses. "On your eighteenth birthday, everyone in the pack was given the mission to take your life for our queen. Only a few accepted because the rest of us understand that peace is better than the hatred that has existed between our people all these long years." His gaze shifts to each of my mates. "The reputation of your guards is known far and wide. This alone deters many from seeking to take your life."

"Why does the wolf queen keep him there?"

His gaze shifts to my mates. "It is forbidden to bring a human to our kingdom, across the veil. She will not break her own laws. Not even to imprison one she considers her enemy."

"And why has she not killed him?" Kai asks.

"That, I do not know," he replies.

My mates all turn to me. Devon's voice fills my mind. "*I do not trust him. He is wolf kind. He could be an agent of the queen.*"

Kai nods. "*I agree. We should not trust him.*"

Nyx looks to us. "*What if he is telling the truth? A wolf would make a good ally. The queen will have the prince heavily guarded in the tower.*"

I touch Nyx's arm. *"Can you use a spell like you did with the wolf shifter in the woods? See if he is speaking the truth?"*

He shakes his head. *"No."* His brown eyes sweep to the wolf shifter. *"He is skilled in magic. I can smell it on him. There would be no way for me to know if he counteracts my spell should I use it to see if he is telling the truth."*

"The wolf queen is bound to have many patrolling Ella's home," Cash interrupts. *"As much as I hate to admit it, we may not be enough to rescue the prince if we go in there alone."*

"What about the humans?" Finn asks. *"The king and queen might send guards to help us."*

I shake my head. *"The king does not trust us enough to commit his guards. That he asked us to bring back his son is a test. And if we fail, I'm certain he will hunt us down."* I pause. *"We have no choice but to trust this man. If we are to have any chance, we will need more help."*

Devon looks to me. *"No. We should not trust him. We can do this alone."*

I take his hand. *"No, we can't. Not if we want everyone to make it through this alive."* I look to the rest of my mates. *"I do not want to lose any of you."*

Kai lowers his head. *"Unfortunately, she is right. We will need help if we are to succeed."*

Devon clenches his jaw as he looks at us. *"You are all fools who will be killed the moment this male double-crosses us."*

Kai's gaze burns with anger as he looks to Devon. *"I am the leader here, and Ella says we should trust him. She is the one who makes the final decision on this. Not you."*

He growls low in his throat as he grits his teeth. *"Fine."*

We turn back to the wolf shifter. Kai steps forward. "Gather any who are loyal to our cause and have them meet us at the edge of the forest. We will move at dawn to rescue the prince."

The man bows again then leaves.

CHAPTER 33

ELLA

I t doesn't take long to get back to our cottage. When we do, Cash, Finn, Nyx, and Kai leave to patrol the barrier while Nyx fortifies it with his magic, leaving me alone with Devon.

He refuses to look at me or even speak as he lies on the couch, feigning indifference to the entire world.

I walk over to him. "Are you done brooding?"

He lifts his gaze to me, his eyes burning with frustration, but he says nothing.

"Is this how you're going to treat me every time we disagree?"

Again, he remains silent as he stares up at me.

"You know what?" I snap. "I'm used to being ignored and being treated like I'm less than a person." Tears well up in my eyes, but I blink them back, biting my bottom lip to stop it from trembling. "So, I guess this is nothing new for me."

With that, I turn and march up the stairs, angry at him for being so stubborn.

As soon as I reach the bedroom, the first tear escapes my lashes as dark memories of my time with my stepmother surface in my mind. She never cared for my feelings either. I was not even a person to her; I was merely a thing. A tool to be used to serve her and her daughter. Unable to hold them back, tears begin streaming down my face. I collapse on the bed, burying my head in my pillow to muffle the sounds of my crying.

I hate that Devon is angry with me. Why does he have to be this way? Anything could happen to us tomorrow, and I don't want to leave here mad at one another. Especially since it could be the last time we ever have a chance to speak.

Warm hands grip my shoulders, but I shrug them away, knowing it's Devon. He grips me a bit more firmly and pulls me up into his lap.

I push against his chest, not wanting him to see my tears, but he holds me tightly to him.

"Let me go!"

"No, I will not."

I struggle a moment, but he grips my chin firmly, tipping my head up to look at him. His green eyes meet mine. His vertically slit pupils contracting and expanding as he stares down at me. Tenderly, he brushes the hair back from my face and wipes at my tears with his thumb as he cups my cheek. I look down, refusing to meet his eyes.

"Look at me," he commands.

Shaking my head, I keep my gaze lowered.

"Look at me, Ella," he growls.

My eyes snap up to meet his. "Why?" I ask, tipping my chin up in defiance. "I don't want to see you angry at me. I don't want that to be the last image I have of you in my mind in case I—"

"In case what?" he asks in a low voice.

I clench my jaw. "In case I die tomorrow."

His eyes widen slightly in alarm. "You will not be going anywhere near the estate tomorrow. We will not allow you to place yourself in danger. You will not die tomorrow, Ella. My vow."

I shake my head. "I'm not letting you all go by yourselves. I can't just stay behind while you put yourselves in danger."

He clenches his jaw. "You can and you will," he snarls.

I jerk my chin from his grasp and push at his chest.

He responds by tightening his arms around me.

"Let me go!"

"I am your guard, and it's my duty to keep you safe. I won't let you go."

I turn back to him, anger burning inside me at his stubbornness. "Why?"

His green eyes stare deep into mine. "Because I love you, Ella."

I go still as his gaze holds mine.

He leans in then gently skims the tip of his nose alongside mine as he whispers. "I love you more than anything in this entire world, even if you do not love me. I vow that I will do whatever it takes to keep you safe, my Ella."

When he pulls back, his expression is so vulnerable and full of pain, it breaks me. I reach up and cup his cheek. "Why do you think I don't love you?"

He lowers his gaze. "Because you have already chosen everyone but me. And I am a cat shifter. My nature alone would give any pause to take me as theirs. So, I do not blame you for not wanting me."

"What do you mean 'your nature'?" I furrow my brow in confusion. "I don't understand."

"My people are known for their possessive nature, more so than many of the other shifters. When we... take our mates, we mark them."

"Mark them how?" I ask, curious to understand.

"When we mate, we bite our partners." He lowers his gaze as if ashamed. "Many fear us because of this. They believe we are more animal than man. They even point to our eyes to prove this theory. And..." he sighs heavily, "perhaps they are right."

I reach up and trace the sharp line of his brow as I stare deep into his cat-like eyes. "Your eyes are beautiful, Devon." I take his hand and entwine our fingers. Lifting them to my chest, I place our joined hands over my heart. "I love you, Devon. Just as much as I love the others."

I press a kiss to the back of his hand between his thumb and forefinger. "I want you to seal me to you before tomorrow. I want to be yours before you go."

He stares down at me like I'm a rare and precious thing. "You choose me to be your mate?"

"Yes, Devon. I want you."

He crushes his lips to mine in a searing kiss, stealing the breath from my lungs.

When he pulls back, his eyes search mine. "I overheard what you told Nyx."

I stare up at him in confusion.

"About humans and their cycles," he explains.

My cheeks heat in embarrassment. If he heard that, then he heard everything else we did that day. "You were there?" I ask in shock.

He swallows thickly. "I was worried and searching for you. I left as soon as I realized and I—"

I press my finger to his lips to silence him. "Why are you telling me this? What does what I told Nyx have to do with anything?"

"I will take great care to make certain you never become pregnant with my child. Most females not of my kind do not want cat shifter children, and I will never ask you to—"

I quiet him with a kiss. Wrapping my arms tightly around

his neck, I hold him close. He groans as I curl my tongue around his, deepening our kiss.

When I pull away, I gently rest my forehead to his as I stare at him intently. "I would gladly bear a child to any one of you," I tell him. A shy smile curves my lips as my cheeks flush with warmth. "With five of you, it's inevitable that I will get pregnant someday."

He shakes his head softly. "But I could be sure to remove myself from your body before I—"

"No." I state firmly. "I want all of you. Isn't that how it works anyway? To be sealed, I have to accept your essence deep inside me."

He nods. "Yes, but I would be content just to have you, Ella."

"But I wouldn't be. I want everything you would give me, Devon."

He wraps his arms tightly around me and captures my mouth in a claiming kiss. His mouth is warm, and he tastes of the forest as his tongue strokes against mine. He allows the illusion of his clothes to disappear, leaving him completely naked beneath me as he holds me in his lap.

His cock is a rigid bar against my core. Only the thin barrier of my clothing separates us.

His kisses become more urgent as his hands travel up and down my form. He grasps the neckline of my dress and pulls it down to reveal my bare chest. The fabric tears as he lowers it even further to cup my breast.

When he rips his mouth from mine, I already miss his taste. But when he closes his lips over my breast and begins an urgent suction, a low moan escapes me.

I thread my fingers through his hair, holding him close to me as he lavishes attention on my breasts with his mouth and his hands.

His touch is a bit rough compared to the others, but I find

I don't care. And when he lifts his eyes to stare up at me, his gaze is fiery and possessive, making the muscles of my core ache with want for him to fill me.

His nostrils flare, and he growls low in arousal. "I can scent your need, my mate."

His hand trails up my thigh until he reaches the triangular scrap of material that covers me. I gasp as he fists it in his hand and tears it from my body.

He dips his fingers through my already slick folds. And as soon as he finds the small pearl of flesh at the apex, I throw my head back and moan out his name.

"You are perfect, Ella," he growls. "And you are mine."

"Yours," I agree as I drag my nails down his back. "I want you, Devon. I want you inside me."

Without warning, my head hits the pillow as he throws me back onto the bed. I only have a moment to be surprised before he lowers his head between my thighs and drags his tongue through my folds.

I inhale sharply, as he teases his tongue at my sensitive flesh and inserts one finger into my core. "So tight," he moans against me. "I don't want to hurt you when I take you."

"You won't," I barely manage to breathe. "Devon, I—" My breath catches as pleasure coils so tightly within me it chases away all rational thought. Fire ignites inside me, and I arch up against him a moment before my release roars through me so intense I cry out his name.

I haven't even caught my breath before his large hands grip my waist and flip me onto my stomach. He covers me immediately. The large crown of his cock bumps against my core as he bands an arm around my waist and drags me toward him.

His tongue traces along the curve of my neck and

shoulder as he grazes his sharp fangs across my sensitive flesh. Arousal spikes through me.

"You are mine," he growls against my skin. "My beautiful Ella."

I release a choked cry as he sinks his fangs deep into my neck and thrusts his cock deep in my channel. Stars explode behind my eyes, and I moan as he begins pumping into me.

With his mouth clamped down on my neck and his arm wrapped up under my hips, he holds me in place as each stroke becomes deeper and more forceful. It's almost more than I can take, and just when I think I'm going to come, he pulls me up to sitting as he continues to thrust up into me.

His grip is almost bruising on my hips as he growls against my neck. This new angle makes everything that much more sensitive as he sinks impossibly deeper inside me, stretching me almost to the point of pain but not quite.

I reach back and run my fingers through his hair while I grip his arm tightly with my other hand.

His hand moves from my hip to my mons, teasing the sensitive hooded flesh at the apex of my folds. It's too much. My body goes tight as a bowstring, and I fall over the edge.

His cock pulses strongly. Intense heat erupts inside me as he fills me with his essence. The small muscles of my channel clamp down around him, pulling his seed deep into my womb as waves of pleasure move through me so intense I cry out his name.

As I come down from my climax, he kisses along my neck, tracing his tongue over the small puncture marks left behind by his fangs. I reach up and feel as they close beneath my fingers. I twist my head to look at him. "How did you do that?"

He nuzzles my cheek as a deep rumbling growl vibrates through his chest. "It is part of the marking of our mates," he whispers. "We can close the mating wound. Don't worry. The

ARIA WINTER & JADE WALTZ

mark will only be visible to any shifter's eyes and not your kind."

He carefully lays us down on our sides, skimming his fingers along my body and down my thigh before moving back up to cup my breast.

He kisses a lazy trail along my neck as he brushes his thumb over the already stiff peak. I reach back and run my fingers through his hair as I moan his name.

His hand moves down my body to cup my mons possessively. "I want you again, Ella. I need you." He runs his delicious tongue over my ear before lightly nipping at my neck.

When he takes me again, I marvel at his complete mastery over my body. His touch is almost too much for me to take, and just when I think I will break from such intense pleasure, he pulls back just enough to keep me right where he wants me: on the razor-sharp edge of my desire.

His intense gaze holds mine as he pumps into me. He drops down low, wrapping his arms around my back as he clamps his mouth down on my neck. I love the sensation of being pinned beneath him like this as he holds me in place. My fingers dig into his back, feeling the muscles flex and extend beneath my fingers as he thrusts hard and deep.

When I come, it's with a keening cry. It triggers his release. His cock pulses in my channel, flooding me with delicious warmth as he comes deep inside me.

He takes me so many times I lose count. And when I'm falling asleep, I'm completely enveloped in his warmth as he curls himself protectively around me. He brushes the hair back from my face and whispers into my ear. "I love you, my beautiful Ella."

"I love you too, Devon," I reply as I drift off to sleep.

CHAPTER 34

DEVON

I stare down at my beautiful mate as she sleeps in my arms. I shift slightly, and she instinctively nestles closer against me. Ella is perfect, and I love her more than anything in this world. That is why what I do now is so hard.

I must leave her. I do not trust the wolf shifter from the store, and I do not trust Ella to stay behind when we are supposed to go in the morning. She is determined to come with us. Kai is too weak and vulnerable to her charms to refuse her anything, even something as dangerous as this.

I suspect he would take her with us to the edge of the forest then leave one or two of us behind with her, but I do not even want her that close to the estate and the trap I know is set to spring the moment we enter.

Nor do I want her to lose more than one of us. So, if anyone is going to risk their life, it should be me. I have always been more of an outsider than any of the others. It is in my nature to be this way and not because I dislike my bond brothers. In truth, I love them all—more than the family I was born into. They are as much my brothers as my flesh and blood, and I refuse to let any of them risk their lives on this foolish mission.

The wolf shifter's eyes appeared as if he were speaking the truth, but I will not wager anyone's life but my own that this is correct. I will go to the estate and save the prince—or die trying.

I refuse to allow anyone else to get hurt or risk their life, especially in a situation forced upon us.

Carefully, I untangle myself from my mate and stand from the bed. I lean down and press a tender kiss to Ella's temple. "I will always love you, my beautiful Ella," I whisper in her ear.

I quietly make my way down the stairs and find four pairs of eyes staring up at me. Kai gives me a questioning look. "Where are you going?"

I meet his gaze evenly. "I'm going to the estate to free the prince."

"We will go with you," Cash says, stepping forward.

"No," I growl. "You will all stay behind with Ella. You must protect her."

"We agreed to all go together," Finn says. "The plan is to go to the edge of the forest at dawn."

I shake my head. "It is a trap, and you know it. All of you." I look at them. "Can you not feel it in your heart that something isn't right?"

Finn nods. "I sense something, but I am... uncertain what it is." He places a hand on my shoulder. "But you should not go alone. I will go with you."

"No. I don't want anyone else to risk their lives on this mission. If I do not return, you will know it was a trap. You must do whatever you can to keep Ella safe."

Cash's eyes are full of sadness. "What would you have us

tell her? You have only just sealed yourself to her and now you leave?"

I clench my jaw. "Tell Ella that I love her and ask for forgiveness."

"You stupid cat," Nyx hisses. "Reckless as always."

My head snaps toward him, and I narrow my eyes as I growl low. "What did you say, rabbit?"

"I said"—Nyx steps forward, tipping his chin up haughtily —"you are stupid if you think you are going alone."

"He's right," Kai says. "At least one of us should go with you."

My heart squeezes in my chest as my bond brothers stare at me, their eyes full of loyalty and devotion. I lower my gaze. "I do not want any of you to get hurt."

"And do you think we do not wish for your safety as well, brother?" Nyx says. He turns to Kai. "I will go with him."

I open my mouth to argue, but Kai nods his head. "Do not engage anyone. Simply scout the area. If it does not appear to be a trap, we can come for the prince tonight or tomorrow instead."

Nyx claps a hand on my shoulder and nods. He looks to me. "You ready?"

"As ready as I'll ever be."

He arches a condescending brow then shifts. *"Try to keep up, cat."*

Together, we race through the forest and toward the estate.

CHAPTER 35

DEVON

The first of the sun's rays barely peak above the horizon by the time we reach the estate. Quietly, we approach the garden wall, hiding behind some bushes, when we see two wolf shifters walking toward the tower door, disappearing inside.

We wait a moment longer for anyone else but see no one. I turn to Nyx. "It is guarded, but not heavily. This is strange, is it not?"

A deep feeling of unease moves through me as I scan the area again. *"Whatever this trap is, I already feel as if we're as good as dead the minute we enter the tower."*

Nyx remains silent, his brow furrowed deeply. After a moment, his voice fills my head. *"How many times?"*

I cock my head to the side in confusion. *"What?"*

"How many times did you bring her to completion?"

I clench my jaw. *"More than you."*

His brows rise slightly, and he smirks. *"I doubt that."*

I growl low in my throat.

"I'll bet if we asked her, she'd say that I am the better lover."

I narrow my eyes. *"Why are you bringing this up now?"*

A grin tugs at Nyx's lips. *"Would you care to wager a bet?"*

"A bet?"

"Yes."

"On what?"

"On who can make her come more times in one hour."

I give him an incredulous look. *"Are you trying to make me mad?"*

"No. I could sense your despair just a moment ago." Nyx chuckles softly and claps a hand on my shoulder. *"I am merely giving you a reason to live."*

Before I can reply, he adds. *"All right. Let's go."*

I scowl after him, and we move toward the tower.

A cool breeze rushes toward us, and we stop just outside the door. My nostrils flare, and alarm bursts through me. *"Do you scent that?"* I ask Nyx.

He nods. *"Death."*

"Yes, but whose?"

"Hopefully not the prince," he replies.

As we carefully make our way up the stairs, it feels like forever until we reach the door to Ella's old bedroom. Everything is so drafty, cold, and run down. I hate that this was her home for so many years.

My heart aches with the want to hold and kiss her, to bury myself deep in her warmth and hear her cry out in pleasure—but all that must wait. I must remain sharp, for I do not intend to die here.

I look to Nyx and nod. As one, we burst through the door only to stop in confusion when we do not see the wolf shifters and instead find only the prince, his body bound as he lies on the floor.

Next to him were three familiar females that belonged to none other but Ella's stepfamily. Bruises and cuts cover their skin, paired with the fear etched upon their faces, could mean only one thing.

They were brutally murdered and left lying to rot in the very room they had forced Ella, the true owner of the estate, to live.

I despise them for their treatment of her, and I had wanted, at one time, even to kill them myself. But as I look to them, I am reminded that death is such a terrible and awful thing for any creature, no matter how evil.

Scrunching my nose to try to hide the horrid stench, I rush toward the lost prince and remove the gag from his mouth. "Where is everyone else?"

"Are you here to save me?" he asks, his eyes wide with what I recognize as hope.

I nod. "Now, answer the question."

He shrugs. "There hasn't been anyone here since last night."

I spin back to Nyx and give him a curious look.

His nostrils flare as he scents the air. "Magic," he growls low under his throat. "The guards were not real. They were decoys."

"Decoys?" I frown. "But why?"

My heart stops then begins pounding as panic coils tight in my chest. "The cottage," I barely manage. "We have to leave! Hurry!"

"But the prince," Nyx says. "The prophecy says he must kill the queen."

I rush to his side and shred his binding with my claws, freeing him.

He stands and rubs at his wrists, raw and bleeding from the tight ropes. He looks at us. "I do not know who you are, but thank you. As for the wolf queen,"—he grits through his teeth—"I will find her, and I will kill her for keeping me prisoner. I am a prince, and I will not allow this crime to go unpunished."

"Fine," I tell him. "Now, climb onto me."

"Climb?" he asks, but then his jaw drops as I partially shift into my much larger cat-like form. Large enough for both him and Nyx to climb on.

"Let's go!" I project to Nyx, knowing the prince cannot hear me while I'm in this form.

Nyx looks to him. "He's telling us to hurry. Let's go."

I'm glad the prince doesn't ask any more questions because there isn't time. I suppose having been held for all this time by shifters, he's seen enough of them transform that it is no longer such a shock to him as it was the first time he saw it.

CHAPTER 36

ELLA

I wake up surrounded by two sets of strong arms wrapped solidly around me. Opening my eyes, I look up to see Finn, and I know without looking back that Cash is behind me.

Finn reaches out and tucks a stray tendril of hair behind my ear. He presses a tender kiss to my forehead. His gaze drifts down to my neck, and he gives me a pained look. "Oh, Ella," he says softly as his fingers trace over the place where Devon marked me. "Are you hurt?"

"No, I'm fine." I glance over his shoulder. "Where is Devon?" I grin teasingly at Finn. "Did you two crowd him out?"

Finn's eyes are serious as they stare across at me, and he shakes his head. "He left, Ella."

Small tendrils of fear begin to unfurl deep inside me as dread settles in my gut. I turn to look at Cash. "Where did he go?"

"To free the prince."

I jerk up. "Devon went by himself?" I ask alarmed.

"No," Cash says. "Nyx went with him."

"But I thought we were all supposed to go. Why did they leave by themselves?"

Kai walks into the bedroom. "They are simply going to scout it out to determine if it is a trap."

"It's too dangerous," I counter. "How could you just let them go alone like that?"

Kai stares at me, his eyes full of guilt. "Forgive us, Ella. We are merely trying to protect you."

"I don't care about myself," I protest. "I care about all of you! I don't want to lose you! Any of you!"

He takes my hand. "And that is how we all feel about you, my Ella. We are your guards. We would die to keep you safe."

"I don't want you to die," I snap.

I get out of bed and move to the closet, grab some clothes, and quickly pull them on.

"Ella," Finn says. "They should be back soon. Do not—"

"Don't tell me not to worry," I say quickly. "We need to go find them. Now."

They each stare at me, pity visible behind their eyes. I turn and rush down the stairs. I'm not sure how I'll cross the veil, but I will. I'll find a way. I can't just stay here while Nyx and Devon put their lives at risk to save the prince. I promised the king and queen we would save him, and I won't let them die for a vow that I made.

Kai, Finn, and Cash storm down the stairs after me.

"Ella, wait!" Cash calls out.

I spin to face them.

A loud boom splits the air behind me, and the door flies inward. Kai, Cash, and Finn rush toward me, pulling me quickly behind them as a wolf steps inside.

It shifts into a beautiful woman with deep red eyes.

Although I've never seen her before, I'm sure this is the wolf queen.

A moment later, my suspicions are confirmed when two men walk in behind her. "My queen," one of them says. "Let us handle this for you."

"No," she growls. Her lips pull back in a feral snarl as she stares across at me. "I must be the one to do it. I will rip her throat out myself. The prophecy ends today."

Ice fills my veins as she stalks toward us. As she moves closer, more of her men come in from outside.

"How did you find us?" Kai asks.

She gives him an evil grin. "Are you referring to that pitiful magical barrier?" She huffs. "This is my kingdom. Did you really believe you could hide yourselves from me?"

There are too many. Kai, Cash, and Finn will die trying to protect me, and I cannot allow that to happen. I'm dead anyway; I don't want them to die too.

I meet the queen's eyes evenly, tipping up my chin to appear unafraid. The slight tremble of my hands betrays me, so I curl them into fists at my side to still their shaking. "Don't hurt them! It's me you want. Not them."

She narrows her eyes. "You offer yourself as sacrifice in their stead?"

"Yes," I state firmly. "I do."

Finn growls low in his throat. "If any of you dare try to harm my mate, I will end you," he grits through his teeth.

The queen's eyes widen slightly in surprise. "You are her mate?"

He looks at her but says nothing. Her gaze shifts to me. "A human took a shifter as her mate?" she asks, and I note the hint of skepticism in her voice.

"I love them," I tell her. "All of them. And yes, they are mine, and I am theirs."

She throws her head back and laughs. It's an evil, guttural

sound that sends fear skittering up my spine. She looks back at me, a smirk twisting her lips. "You really have mated them all, haven't you? Oh, this is completely unexpected." She tips her head to the side in an almost thoughtful look. "It seems I'm saving the prince from much heartache and grief. He would not have wanted to share you, my dear."

"I don't want the prince," I tell her. "I never did."

She shrugs. "Well, then I suppose I'm doing you a favor by sparing you from completing the prophecy."

A loud cry draws our attention back to the door. Two of the queen's men turn toward it and rush outside. The sounds of fighting ring out a moment before Devon, Nyx, and the prince rush through the door. Each of them covered in blood.

The queen growls low in her throat. "How dare you kill my pack!"

Devon narrows his eyes. "They are not all dead. Some are merely unconscious. If you want to live to see them, you will leave here. Now," he grinds out.

Without warning, she rushes toward me. Her movements so fast, her image is a blur as she crosses the room. I've been around it enough to recognize magic when I see it. This must be her particular skill. I blink and then I'm staring at a mirror image of myself.

My jaw drops as her eyes meet mine.

CHAPTER 37

FINN

I've heard how powerful the queen's magic is, but I have never seen her use it before. Lightning fast, she races past us, and when we spin, we find two versions of Ella.

But which one is real, and which one is the queen?

We don't have time to find out. Together, we rush them both. Cash, Kai, and Nyx grab one, while Devon, the prince, and I hold the other.

"The mark!" Devon's voice cries out in our minds.

I look at them both and realize the other one is missing the mating mark from Devon.

Cash, Kai, Nyx, and Devon growl and tear into her. She releases a pained cry as she twists away from their grasp. When she spins back to face them, she's wielding a knife that she must have summoned with her magic.

With the blade raised before her, she rushes toward Ella in a blur of speed. Time slows, almost standing still as the prince jumps in front of her, taking the impact.

He cries out as the queen buries the knife deep into his side.

She climbs over him to reach Ella, and I watch in shock as Ella pulls the blade from the prince's torso and sinks it deep into the queen's chest.

Her eyes go wide in shock as she stares down at the blade's handle. She grips it firmly and pulls it from her chest. Blood gushes down her front and pools at her feet.

The queen drops to her knees then collapses on the floor.

A great howling cry comes from the door, followed by several others.

"What are they doing?" Ella asks.

Two of the wolf shifters enter and drop before her on one knee. "Long live the queen," he says solemnly to Ella.

We watch in awe as each of them bows to her, pledging fealty. It is an old law among our kind. If our ruler falls in battle, the crown goes to the victor.

The Elders said the prophecy showed them it would be the prince who would do this—but instead, it is Ella. She is the rightful queen of our people now. To unite the two kingdoms, she must marry the prince.

I turn to my brothers, their eyes full of sadness, and I realize they must have reached the same conclusion as me.

We look at Ella. She is holding the prince's head in her lap as he stares up at her, his eyelids fluttering open and closed. She takes his hand. "Don't worry," she says. "We are going to save you, my prince."

CHAPTER 38

ELLA

The same healing balm that was used on my injuries works for the prince as well. I watch in awe as Finn spreads it over his wound, and the tissue begins to knit back together. As soon as it's finished, Devon transforms so that he can carry the prince on his back and return him to the castle.

Everyone is quiet as we make our way there. It still has not fully hit me yet that I am now the queen of the shifter kingdom. I left instructions with one of the wolves to inform everyone that the old queen is dead.

He bowed low, crossing his arm over his chest before leaving.

"Do you think we can trust them?" I asked Kai.

He nodded. "It is the law. They must obey. The magic binds them to the crown, regardless of who wears it."

He gives me a pained smile, and I reach out and cup his cheek. "What is wrong? Why are you looking at me like that?"

A tear slips down his cheek. "Whatever happens, we will always remain your guards, Ella."

I stare up at him in confusion. "What do you mean? What are you talking about?"

He opens his mouth to answer but stops when one of the king's guards steps forward. His eyes go wide as soon as he sees the prince on Devon's back.

"The prince has returned!" he calls out, and nearby guards behind him surround the prince as a servant rushes back toward the palace to inform the king and queen.

When we reach the throne room, the queen rushes forward and embraces her son. "My son! You are alive!" she cries out. "Thank the heavens!"

I step forward. "Your son has been returned to you as promised. Now, I ask of you: Will we now have peace with the shifters?"

The king stands. "We will discuss it with their ruler."

"You already are," Kai says, gesturing to me. He bows low. "Ella killed the wolf queen to save your son. Now she is the ruler of our kingdom."

The king studies me a moment then nods. "Then let us cement an alliance through marriage." He gestures to his son. "Alexander, are you willing to take Ella as your wife?"

Alexander looks to me, his eyes wide. "Without hesitation." He smiles and holds his hand out to me. "For the betterment of the people of the kingdom."

I notice that Kai and the rest of my mates stand beside me in silence, offering nothing in the way of protest. It hurts. Deeply. I thought that they loved me. Why are they silent now?

I give the king a hesitant look. "No offense to the prince, but what if I do not want to be married?"

His expression grows stern. "This is how alliances are

cemented. A treaty forged only on parchment rarely lasts very long."

He is right. Everyone knows this. Treaties and alliances not bound by marriage fail all the time; it has happened in many other kingdoms abroad. I look back at my mates. I have to think of my people now that I am the queen of the shifter kingdom. Can I condemn them to a life of constant war and hate between the humans and us?

I think of the wolf shifter from the shop. He was willing to risk everything for peace just so that his pack could live without fear. Is that not what a queen does? Sacrifice herself and what she wants for the good of her people?

I look once more at my mates, wondering if any of them will protest, but they remain silent.

I take the prince's hand. "Very well," I tell him. "Let us secure peace between our two kingdoms through marriage."

CHAPTER 39

CASH

Her words hit me like a physical blow. I look to my bond brothers, and it is easy to read the devastation written on their faces. We're all shattered. It will have to be enough to be her guards and no more. We cannot keep her as our mate, not now that she belongs to the prince. Humans do not share.

His sharp gaze travels over Ella with a lustful stare. Yes, I can already see the possessiveness in his eyes as he looks at her. Who can blame him? She is the most beautiful female I have ever seen.

My stomach twists in a violent knot as the king informs them that all they must do to seal their marriage is consummate their bonding. The prince wastes no time leading her away while we watch in despair.

CHAPTER 40

ELLA

As the prince leads me down the hallway to his chambers, I cannot stop feeling like this doesn't seem right. I know I should be willing to sacrifice for my people, but this is asking too much. How can I give up my mates? I love them.

"Alexander, stop," I tell him.

He pulls me inside the bedroom and closes the door.

"There's something I have to tell you," I state firmly.

I cannot do this. I love my mates, and I don't care about treaties or kingdoms. Not if it means I cannot be with them. I'm selfish, and all I want is my mates. I will not marry the prince. I refuse.

He stares at me with a look somewhere between uncertainty and hunger. "I cannot deny that I am attracted to you, Ella. You are the most beautiful woman I have ever seen, but is this what you want as well?" he asks. "I must know because my parents do not have a marriage based on love, and it has not served either of them well. I do not want a match like theirs. One that is based simply on the good of the kingdom."

The prince is a good man. "Then, I must tell you the truth." I meet his gaze evenly. "The men I was with, the ones who saved you... they are my guards, but they are also my mates. I have bound myself to them. I love them, Alexander. And I cannot give them up."

He blinks at me in surprise. "You have bound yourself to shifters?"

"Of course, they are mine."

"But you are human," he says, confusion lacing his tone.

I smile at him. "Appearances matter not in the eyes of love."

He nods. "I understand this." He clears his throat. "Very well. We do not have to marry, you and I."

"But can we still have peace?"

"Yes. I vow we will always have peace between us." He tips his head to the side. "I think I know of a way my father will accept it."

"How?"

He grins. "By promising that we will eventually unite our kingdoms through marriage someday."

I stare at him in confusion.

He continues. "We will tell him that our children will marry when they come of age, thus uniting our two kingdoms."

"And what if they do not wish to?" I ask because I have to know. I will not bind my unborn children to something that even I would be hesitant to accept.

He smiles. "You are already the queen of your people, and I will be king of mine by then." He shrugs. "If our children refuse to marry each other, so be it. We only need to convince my father it will happen someday, and that will be good enough."

I narrow my eyes. "Do I have your word?"

He nods. "You have my vow, Ella." He reaches out and gently lifts a lock of my hair, allowing it to trail over his fingers. "I would have made a good husband to you."

"You will find love," I tell him. "After all, there are many who desire a prince."

He gives me a pained smile. "But they will not be you."

CHAPTER 41

KAI

"I t's that room." I point down the long hallway. "I'm certain of it."

"Hurry, you stupid bird!" Devon hisses. "We have to get to them before it's too late!"

As soon as we reach the door, Cash tries the handle. It opens, and we rush inside to find Ella standing in the middle of the room, talking with the prince.

She blinks up at us, stunned. "What are you—"

I rush toward her and drop to one knee. Everyone else does the same behind me. "Do not marry him, Ella. We cannot let you go. We love you. Please."

Devon lifts his head to her. "There has to be another way to secure peace. You are ours." He growls at the prince. "He cannot have you."

The prince laughs and arches a brow. "Which one of you will father the child that will marry my son? Or my daughter?" he adds. "I hope it is you." He looks to Devon. "Fire like yours would surely strengthen our line."

Devon blinks at him in confusion. "What are you talking about?"

Ella moves forward and takes Devon's hand. "I'm not going to marry the prince. I told him I couldn't forget all my mates." She smiles. "I love all of you, and I won't give you up." She looks to the prince. "So we agreed that our children will marry each other when they come of age, cementing an alliance between our two kingdoms."

I look to Ella in alarm. I do not know which of us, if any, will father any children with her. But I cannot bear the thought of shackling the poor child with such a huge weight of responsibility before he or she is ever born. "What if our child does not want to do this?"

The prince nods. "Then, they will not have to. We are simply going to present this to my father to appease him and move forward with the treaty."

A slow grin curves my lips. Ella and the prince are both wise. This is a good solution. I note how his gaze travels over her with a look of intense longing. I feel sorry for him in a way. No one will ever compare to our Ella. And when his eyes meet mine, I know he feels the same.

But I would change nothing, for I refuse to give her up. Not for the prince or anyone else. She belongs with my bond brothers and me.

CHAPTER 42

ELLA

Instead of going straight to the palace to claim my new throne, we return to our cottage. I wanted to spend one more night here in the place that I first fell in love with all of my mates.

Besides, word has already spread that I am the new queen, and the kingdom is stable with the alliance between the humans and us. Duty can wait for one night while I reconnect with my mates.

Kai's eyes meet mine as I stand in the center of the bedroom, and they begin to circle me. "We will claim you as one, according to the ways of our people," he says, his eyes full of hunger.

He reaches out, lifting my nightgown away from my body, and discards it on the floor at my feet.

His hand traces down my neck to cup one breast. I lean into his touch and feel several hands all over me.

Closing my eyes, I sigh in contentment as I feel the gentle caress over my breasts and down my body. Someone cups my mons possessively, and I recognize the deep growl of Devon.

Kai moves toward me and lifts me into his arms and carries me to the large bed.

He carefully places me on the mattress as everyone else gathers around me. He moves over me, and I part my thighs to receive him. His cock is fully erect. Liquid beads on the tip and rolls down his shaft as he stares down at me. "You are so beautiful, Ella. And you are all ours."

He reaches down and runs his fingers through my already slick folds, and I moan at the sensation.

Cash and Finn lie down on either side of me. I watch as Cash closes his mouth over my right breast, and Finn does the same to my left. Kai drops down over me. The crown of his cock bumps lightly against my entrance before he pushes into me. I moan as he rocks his hips back and forth as my body adjusts to his invasion.

Nyx leans down and kisses me long and deep while Devon stands off to the side, staring at me with a hungry gaze as he strokes his length.

Kai strokes long and deep as he stares down at me. I wrap my legs tightly around him, and he groans. "You'll be the end of me, Ella," he breathes.

I laugh softly, and a surprised puff of air escapes him. He growls low in arousal. "You're so tight," he rasps. "I can barely hold back."

I smile up at him as I trace my fingers over his heavily muscled chest. "Then, don't."

His eyes burn with lust as he stares down at me and begins to move faster. His strokes are long and deep. The delicious sensation of being touched all over my body is almost more than I can bear.

Cash and Finn close their mouths over my breasts and

begin a gentle suction, sending ripples of pleasure straight down to my core.

The fullness of Kai's cock buried deep inside me is almost more than I can take. Every muscle in my body goes tense before I fall over the edge. Kai falls with me. His hand holds my hip in an almost bruising grip as he empties himself deep inside me. The delicious warmth spreads through me, and I reach up to cup the back of his neck, pulling his face down to mine for a kiss. He plunders my mouth, and when he pulls away, he smiles down at me. "That was only once, my Ella. We will each take you many times this night."

My toes practically curl at his sultry promise.

When he pulls away from my body, Cash moves over me. I gasp as he impales me in one smooth thrust, seating himself completely inside me. He smiles before capturing my lips.

I wrap my arms around him and kiss him deeply. I moan as he begins a slow and steady rhythm deep inside me. "You feel so good."

He wraps his arms around my back and pulls me up to sitting. I wrap my legs around him and notice that he looks over his shoulder at someone.

I feel Finn behind me a moment later. I recognize his strong hands on my breasts as he pins me between him and his brother. His cock is a hard bar against my backside, and as Cash begins to thrust up into me, Finn presses his length against me as well. I'm worried he'll try to enter me from behind, and I'm not sure I'm ready for that yet.

As if sensing my concern, he leans forward and breathes in my ear. "Do not worry, my Ella. We will save that for later. I will take you after Cash finishes with you."

I lean back against him as he cups my breasts, teasing the hard tips between his thumb and forefinger as he trails his mouth over my neck, leaving suctioning kisses across my skin.

Cash holds me tightly as he thrusts up into me. He looks to his brother and begins to move faster. Each stroke feels stronger and deeper.

The muscles of my channel quiver and flex around his length, and he groans as his cock begins to pulse inside me, filling me with delicious warmth as I cry out his name.

Waves of pleasure are still moving through me, and before I can come down from my high, Cash pulls away from me, and Finn is pushing into my channel. The stretch as he fills my core is almost to the point of pain but not quite. Every nerve in my body is lit up with intense pleasure as Finn pumps up into me, groaning with each thrust.

Cash is still hard. His cock pressing insistently against my abdomen as he moves against me as well.

He leans down and closes his mouth over my breast. I open my mouth, and a low moan escapes me a moment before Kai cups my cheek and turns my head to him, kissing me long and deep.

Nyx is on the other side of me next to Devon, each of them stroking their lengths as they watch me.

Just the sight of them fills me with desire. My body clenches around Finn's length as I find my release, crying out his name. He erupts deep inside me, flooding me with warmth as he fills me with his seed.

Cash groans and presses even harder against me as thick ropes of liquid erupt from his cock, covering my chest and abdomen.

I reach back and cup Finn's neck to bring his lips down to mine. He kisses me before pulling away.

I don't have any time to recover before Nyx bears me down to the mattress. He enters me in one deep thrust, stealing the air from my lungs as he begins a fast and unrelenting rhythm as he pumps into me.

His lovemaking is urgent and frenzied. As if he can barely

hold himself back. I wrap my arms and legs around him tightly, trying to hold on as pleasure coils tight in my core.

My mouth falls open, and I'm panting heavily. He drops down low and wraps his arms tightly around me as his thrusts become faster and deeper. "Oh, Nyx," I barely manage. "I'm already going to—"

My breath catches as every muscle in my body locks up, and I release a keening cry as I come hard. My channel clamps firmly around him, triggering his own release. He roars out my name as his cock pulses hard and deep, flooding my womb with his seed.

He rolls us so that I'm on top while he's still fully seated inside me. He grips my hips firmly as he grinds up into my core. "Nyx," I cry out. "It's too much," I breathe.

"I need you," he grits through his teeth. "I need to fill you again, Ella."

A warm body covers me from behind, and I look back to find Devon. He presses me down so that I'm lying atop Nyx while he moves over me. His cock is hard against my backside.

Nyx begins to move faster until I am gasping and panting over him, barely able to keep my breath.

I cry out as another orgasm moves through me, this one stronger than the last. Intense heat floods me a moment later as he comes inside me with a deep groan.

Devon wraps his arm around my waist as Nyx moves out from under me.

He tugs me back against him, his crown pressing into my entrance. The deep stretch as he fills me is so intense I nearly come right then and there.

He leans down and traces his tongue over my skin as he strokes deep inside me. He pulls me up so that I'm on my hands and knees as he thrusts into me from behind.

I'm so spent my arms and legs feel weak, and it's hard to

keep up with each pump of his hips against mine. I feel as if the best I can do is keep myself upright while he takes me with each thrust.

Kai and Nyx are on either side of me, cupping my breasts. Cash reaches up under me and begins to tease at the small bundle of nerves between my folds, driving me mad with desire.

Finn is in front of me, watching as he strokes his length.

The sight is so erotic, and everything feels so good; I barely feel Devon's teeth as they sink deep into my neck. The sharp edge of pain and pleasure so intense, I cry out as I come hard, the muscles of my channel clamping down around Devon's length.

He thrusts deep as he pins me beneath him. Warmth erupts from his cock, and it's so intense I come again, this time my orgasm seems to go on forever as he fills me with his seed.

Kai moves back down to my side as Devon pulls away. He flips me onto my back and lifts my legs so that my feet are on his shoulders. "I want you again, Ella," he growls low in his throat. "Will you take me?"

Panting heavily, I nod. "I'll take all of you," I allow my gaze to travel over each of them. "Always," I breathe as he slowly enters me.

EPILOGUE

As we stand on the castle's balcony overlooking our kingdom, Kai takes one hand, and Nyx takes the other. Devon stands behind me, wrapping his arms possessively around my waist, while Cash and Finn each place a hand on my shoulders.

The land here has been dry like everywhere else, and I understand now that I can restore it by calling the rain with my song because of my gift. I did not realize that is what I was doing all that time on the estate. But now that I understand this is part of my heritage, I will use it to restore the land both here and in the human kingdom.

My subjects cheer as they stare up at me while I sing, and the rain begins to fall. I am the first human to take shifter mates. The dawn of a new era and a symbol of unity among them and the humans.

Already, our subjects are inquiring about heirs, but all of that can wait until later. Right now, I simply want to govern our kingdom with fairness and enjoy my mates. With each of them beside me, I do not doubt that we can bring prosperity to our people and this land.

I don't know what the future holds for all of us. But as I gaze at my mates, their eyes full of love and devotion, I am happier than I have ever been, and I would not trade this life for anything. They are mine and I am theirs.

ABOUT ARIA WINTER

Thank you so much for reading this. I hope you enjoyed this story. If you enjoyed this book, please leave a review on Amazon (Click Here) and/or Goodreads. I would really appreciate it. Reviews are the lifeblood of Indie Authors.

I have great news! The next book in this RH Fair Tale Series is already listed on Amazon. *Snow White And Her Werewolves*

For information about upcoming releases Like me on Facebook (www.facebook.com/ariawinterauthor) or sign up for upcoming release alerts at my website:

Ariawinter.com

Want more?
Once Upon a Shifter Series
Ella and her Shifters
Snow White And Her Werewolves

Once Upon A Fairy Tale Romance Series
Taken by the Dragon: A Beauty and the Beast Retelling
Captivated by the Fae: A Cinderella Retelling
Rescued By The Merman: A Little Mermaid Retelling
Bound to the Elf Prince: A Snow White Retelling

Cosmic Guardian Series (RH Superhero series)
Charmed by the Fox's Heart
Seduced by the Peacock's Beauty

Protected by the Spider's Web
Ensnared by the Serpent's Gaze
Forged by the Dragon's Flame

Elemental Dragon Warriors Series

Claimed by the Fire Dragon Prince
Stolen by the Wind Dragon Prince
Rescued by the Water Dragon Prince
Healed by the Earth Dragon Prince
Chosen By The Fire Dragon Guard
Saved By The Wind Dragon Guard
Treasured By The Water Dragon Guard
Taken By The Earth Dragon Guard

ABOUT JADE WALTZ

Jade Waltz lives in Illinois with her husband, two sons, and her three crazy cats. She loves knitting, playing video games, and watching Esports. Jade's passions include the arts, green tea and mints — all while writing and teaching marching band drill in the fall.

Jade has always been an avid reader of the fantasy, paranormal and sci-fi genres and wanted to create worlds she always wanted to read.

She writes character driven romances within detailed universes, where happily-ever-afters happen for those who dare love the abnormal and the unknown. Their love may not be easy—but it is well worth it in the end.

Thank you for taking the time to read my book!
Please take a moment to leave a review! <3
Reviews are important for indie self-publishing authors and they help us grow.

Connect with me at:

Facebook Author Page: Jade Waltz
Facebook Group: Jade Waltz Literary Alcove
Twitter: @authorjadewaltz
Instagram: @authorjadewaltz
Email: authorjadewaltz@gmail.com

Project: Adapt
  Found

A failed human prototype. That's all she is…

Born and raised as an experiment, Selena's life has been filled with torture, betrayal, and distrust… but one night changes everything.

Sold, attacked, and on the run, Selena is picked up by a colony ship. Struggling to find her place on this ship and trying to understand the draw she feels toward two alien males, her already uncertain life becomes downright unimaginable when she learns new life is growing inside her.

Terrified her captors will find her and take her and her children back to a life of horror and captivity, she must learn to trust her saviors, and herself.

With the help of her two mates, Selena will fight for her freedom—or die trying.

Found is the first book in a space fantasy alien romance series which will have the heroine travel through the galaxy, experiencing new things and meeting multiple aliens along the way.

Order NOW!

Series Cowritten w/ Aria Winter:

Elemental Dragon Warriors - Alien/Dragon Shifter Romance - MF
Claimed by the Fire Dragon Prince
We set out from Earth in search of a new world. I never thought it would end with us crashing on a planet full of dragon shifters.

When I'm taken from my people by a fierce Drakarian warrior, my first thought is of escape. Varus is the Prince of the Fire Clan. He claims the glowing pattern on his chest means that I'm his fated one—his Linaya.

I doubt he's going to just let me go. But what does it mean to be fated to a dragon?

Read Now!

Cosmic Guardians - Superhero Fantasy Romance - RH

Charmed By The Fox's Heart

When I woke up this morning and went to my regular coffee house, I had no idea my life was about to change forever.

Cael's devastatingly handsome smile and his intense green eyes are swoon worthy enough by themselves, but add in an air of mystery and this guy is the whole package. The excitement I never knew I was missing in my life.

As we grow closer, we find out the fate of two worlds is in our hands. And now we must work together to find allies to prevent a cycle of destruction that could end all life as we know it.

Each time we touch, we feel a connection. I'm drawn to him in ways that I don't understand. For as long as I can remember, I've had a recurring nightmare, and now I find out that Cael has the same dream.

But what does it mean? I know I can trust him with my life, but can I also trust him with my heart?

Read Now!

Once Upon A Shifter - Fantasy Shifter Fairy Tale Retelling Romance – RH
   Ella and Her Shifters
   Snow White And Her Werewolves

www.ingramcontent.com/pod-product-compliance
Lightning Source LLC
Chambersburg PA
CBHW030328200626
46816CB00006BA/1967